WHITE CITY

SEB DOUBINSKY

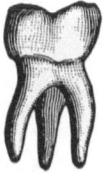

Bizarro Pulp Press
an imprint of JournalStone Publishing

Bizarro Pulp Press books may be ordered through booksellers or by contacting:

Bizarro Pulp Press, a JournalStone imprint
www.BizarroPulpPress.com

ISBN: 978-1-942712-02-2

Printed in the United States of America
JournalStone rev. date: January 12, 2015

Cover Art: Matthew Revert
Interior Formatting by: Lori Michelle
www.theauthorsalley.com

PRAISE FOR *WHITE CITY*

Doubinsky takes us on yet another surreal jaunt into the abyss, this time showcasing the interlinked denizen of Viborg City—an artless and decadent principality on the edge of nowhere. Its ideals are antiquated and the people living there are empty vessels stuck in perpetual melee, desperately trying to find something meaningful (specifically, a news reporter, a writer and a recently transferred cop).

White City is Doubinsky's pragmatic approach to the surreal noir novella, a Babylonian parable about success, greed and, ultimately, loss, all executed with a measured hand and structured with his trademark palpable intelligence—Seb's take on the nature of a wealthy, spoiled writer is particularly enjoyable, self-effacing and poignant. As is often the case with his work, Doubinsky confronts notions of the gender politics, immigration, nationalism, tier systems and, of course, the subjective devices used in dealing with regret.

I wholeheartedly believe it to be a master work of bizarro science fiction and should be read as widely and emphatically as his more sprawling efforts.

This is the yardstick of quality ladies and gentlemen.

—Chris Kelso
author of *The Black Dog Eats the City*
& *The Dissolving Zinc Theatre*

"In the fiction of the brilliant writer Seb Doubinsky, society is bleached squeaky clean. If one is not too ambitious one can enjoy the simplicity and banality and even pleasures of a culture that hums along. One can lose himself in the beautiful symmetry of meticulous bureaucracy, the harmony. Everything is clean and works perfectly. For ugly wars are fought elsewhere in places no one has ever heard of or cares about. In the intense and frightening fiction of Seb Doubinsky, a character is in grave danger if he or she thinks independently or displays any real humanity."

—Matt Bialer
author of *Bridges* and *Ascent*

"A terrifying city of the future; a terrific novel about the present."

—Tabish Khair
author of *A Thing About Thugs*
and *How to Fight Islamist Terror from the Missionary Position.*

"Like a quick succession of vicious stabs into the heart of society, *White City* is the kind of book that begs to be reread. Entertaining and thought-provoking."

—Jordan Krall
author of the *False Magic Kingdom* cycle
and *Your Cities Your Tombs*

TO MY FRIEND, TABISH KHAIR.

"All the power of magic, whether black or white, is based on language."
Heinrich Himmler

"Whatever is purely realistic, slice-of-life, which is average, quotidian, doesn't interest me . . . I am fascinated by what is beautiful, strong, healthy, what is living. I seek harmony. When harmony is produced I am happy."
Leni Riefenstahl

1. OUR GENES AFFECT OUR SMELLING CAPACITIES

Leila Bogossian cursed mentally. Another stupid interview about another stupid event concerning stupid people. She was getting tired of that crap. It had been two years now she had joined the reporter staff of VCTV 2, and they had only given her lousy, second-rate jobs.

Sometimes she wondered if her role model, Sheryl Boncoeur, the Ice Queen of BTV, hadn't slept her way to the top. Here, it was impossible: nobody to sleep with. A bureaucratic hierarchy changing every six months. New names, new faces, new bosses, same old routine. Welcome to Viborg City Television, Channel 2. People said that when you worked in private corporations instead of the public service, it was freedom and efficiency first. That's what she had believed too, and the reason why she had so desired to work there. Yeah, right. There sure was more to the corporate image than met the eye . . . Still, she wanted her career to move upwards and was ready to eat a lot of shit to get there. A ton of it even. And it didn't have to taste like chocolate either.

"Sure, I'll do it," Leila answered Lene Andersen, a blonde bitch from blonde hell and her current boss. Smiling too. Sheryl Boncoeur would have been proud of her, if she had been still alive and made her way to Viborg City, which she had probably never visited in her entire journalistic life.

Lene nodded briefly, without a smile, and turned on her high heels to walk out of the open space office crowded with computers and stressed reporters.

Leila let out a sigh, and sent a text message to Maria, her assigned cameraman.

Some said she was stuck with local news because she was of Samarqandi origin, and that the high-ups didn't want too much "diversity" on national. But she didn't buy that. Her father, a journalist himself, had been a political refugee, always loyal to Viborg City and the

Western Cities' Alliance in his editorials on his website. He had believed in this city, and had passed on the same faith to his daughter, even if his life had been tough. He had worked hard here, first as a cab driver, then as manager for a small Samarqandi take-away restaurant. He had died of cancer a few months after she had graduated from journalist school. It was sad, but at least, he had died proud of his daughter and full of hope for her future.

Well, a good thing he didn't see her now.

A two-note melody told her Maria had answered her message.

"See you in the parking lot."

Efficient, Maria, as usual.

The short-haired fat blonde video technician and the half-monkey anchorwoman. Perfect crew. Minorities unite! She wondered if it was a coincidence. Leila smiled at her own paranoia attack as she got up to leave. Sheryl Boncoeur had been a famous lesbian, and had made it to the top. Too bad she hadn't been black.

LEE JR.

Lee Jones Jr. shut his cell phone and stared for a few long seconds at the near empty street below his small apartment. It was always like that after talking with the old man—his mind went blank.

All the walls were made of red brick and the windows had white panes. The long street was red and white, like Viborg City's national flag. He wondered if the people here dreamed in red and white. Sometimes this city scared him.

His thoughts floated back to his father. Lee Jones Sr., the "Famous Writer," had told his son he had been to Viborg City in his youth. Had fallen in love with a sweet little blonde and had stayed there for a couple of months. Then, as usual, he had got tired of everything and moved on to somewhere else. New Lisbon, New Madrid, somewhere sunny. He had always loved the sun. That's why he lived in New Petersburg now, in a huge condo, by the sea. He had sounded sober on the phone. For once. It was a nice change. Maybe his dad's new wife, whom he had never met, had some influence on this. What was her name again? Maria? Marcia? He didn't dare ask. Enough bad vibes between daddy and sonny. No need to add kerosene to the sleeping embers.

He hadn't mentioned to him either that his last novel, *The Dark Covenant*, was on the bestseller list in New Babylon. His father had fled the city in his youth, tired of the "young wonder" image that suffocated him. And he, the prodigal son . . . He could see his father's scorn from here. For Lee senior, New Babylon embodied all the evil and superficiality of this world. Lee junior couldn't really disagree, but still— that's where the money was. And being able to live in Viborg City, one of the most expensive places on this planet, was direct proof of that. It was a small and cozy flat in the H.C. Andersen district, but it still cost as much as a comfortable condo in Petersburg or even Babylon.

He grabbed a non-filter cigarette from the package on the dining table, absent-mindedly tapping an end against the wooden surface. He had never read one of his father's books. Well, he had actually begun

some of them, but it had been too strange an experience, with his father's grumbly voice superimposing his own inside his brain. He had resented stumbling upon a sex scene. That might explain why he had stopped *War and Pieces* at page 27. Which had been a good 27 pages, actually, he had to admit. Reluctantly.

SIGRID.

"Welcome to White City, Detective-Inspector Wulff" Commissioner Sven Møltke said, leading her into a small office. "I hope you will find it to your liking."

The use of the district's derogatory nickname made Sigrid wonder if it was a subtle hint to show her that he actually was on her side. Møltke had read her files, no doubt. And it was very clear why she was here. "Insubordination." "Reluctance to work with others." "Conflict-prone." All that, underlined in red in the report's conclusion. She knew it by heart. Still burned in her soul like a recent scar.

"All the codes to access the computer are printed on this page. If you have any questions, you can ask Stig. He's been here for a while. He should be able to help you."

Stig Jørgensen was the inspector with whom she was sharing the tiny office. At least it wasn't an open-space, like in the Sorgbjerg station. She would only have to face Stig if she fucked up, not twenty angry faces. Jørgensen wasn't in the office at the moment: His chair was empty, facing a dead computer. There was no coat hanging on the wall hangers.

As if he read her mind, Møltke explained:

"He just had a baby. He's on paternal leave for five weeks. That's the second week now."

Sigrid nodded. Three weeks of calm, she thought. Good.

"Okay," the commissioner said, rubbing his hands as if he had made a good deal. "I guess you're set. There will be a briefing in the meeting room at eleven. See you then."

He left the room, closing the door behind him. Sigrid hung her coat on the back of her chair. There were a couple of files on her desk. She picked one up. A burglary. She picked the two others. More burglaries. Of course. She sighed. Welcome to White City indeed.

Leila.

When Leila arrived in the TV station's parking lot, Maria had already packed her camera in the trunk.

"Ready?" she asked her anyway.

Maria nodded and climbed in the driver's seat. A few seconds later, they were driving out of the station's steel gates, which always reminded Leila of a prison.

"You know the way?" she asked Maria.

She had rarely gone to the Kong Kristian district, which was the Cash area of the city. No reason why she should have: nothing ever happened.

"No, but I've got it on the QuickNav."

It was difficult to have a conversation with Maria. She never said much, just nodded and did the things she was supposed to do. Never anything more.

"I hope it won't rain," Leila said, looking at the grey clouds rolling over the roofs of the red brick city.

Maria gave a quick glance and shrugged. Leila sighed inside. This was going to be a long day.

Dog Poem #1

Everybody smells of piss
Even just a little bit
This poem
Is about that

SIGRID.

Sigrid left her office to explore the rest of the Kong Kristian district police station. It was large and luxurious, with plenty of small offices and high-tech gadgets everywhere. The kitchen was huge, with four coffee machines brewing in sync. The Sorgbjerg station looked like a slum compared to this. They even had art on the walls here—bad art, albeit, but art nonetheless. The open-space section, next to the kitchen, was exclusively reserved for the dispatchers and for the briefings, as she could deduct from the row of chairs lined up on the other end of the room. It was ironic to think that many of her colleagues from Sorgbjerg would have considered this heaven—and that it was considered hell for her. The higher-ups knew her well: Burglaries and a four-star police station. There couldn't be a worse hell for her than this.

LEE JR.

What Viborg City lacked most, in Lee's eyes, was culture. What he meant by that was culture he could relate to. There was a strange mix here of cheap commercial New Babylon syrup and old stiffened national emblems. Nothing in between and nothing outside. The city prided itself in being *über* modern, and yet clung to archaic models, like royalty, flags, religion and dubious local cuisine. It reminded him, in a way, of New London, but New London had an ancient history of mixed cultures and social unrest—as well as a true sense of humor.

Lee turned off the TV—he had been watching a re-run of some ancient New Babylon TV series and sighed. He was bored. Bored and uninspired. He decided to go out and take a walk. His girlfriend would come back late afternoon, as usual. She had a job, the girl. He had one too, but that was a little bit more complicated. No salary, no boss, no time frame. And yet, it was a job. There was money in the bank—not a lot, but enough to survive here one or two years if necessary. His agent still liked him. Could definitely have been worse, for a job.

He picked up his jacket and closed the door of the apartment behind him. His father had said once: "The purpose of a writer is to make life seem more complicated than it actually is." Once again, the son of a bitch had been right.

THEORY OF POWER #1

Always crush your enemies with a friendly face. The victim must feel your love and understand that his or her destruction is necessary for your love to bloom at its maximum strength and beauty.

Leila.

As they arrived in the Kong Kristian district, with its nice two story villas and beautifully mowed lawns, Leila felt a sudden pang of envy. She had been raised in the NoCred district, Sorgbjerg, where everything was cheap, but nothing was free. Her father and mother had struggled hard to make ends meet, and had still ended up NoCred, as most of the immigrant population here. That she had finished journalism school had been nothing short of a small miracle, and the same went for her current job. She was Cred now, and proud of it. She rented a small apartment in the H. C. Andersen district, which she shared with her boyfriend. Nothing fancy, but much, much better than the rent-controlled depressing apartment where she had spent her childhood and where her mother still lived.

Leila considered herself happy, albeit frustrated—like most of her fellow Cred citizens. And now she understood why, as they drove along the silent streets of Kong Kristian: to be Cash seemed unattainable. If you wanted to live here, you either had to be born in money, marry into money, or win at the National Lottery, which was still called "National" although it had been privatized ages ago. Or work here as a butler or a maid.

Then again, she understood the need for society to have classes. It was the only way to have a stable, secure society. Viborg City was an old parliamentary kingdom, after all, and they indeed had a king, although he had only symbolic power now. His palace was the greatest tourist attraction. And that, in a way, explained everything about this city's identity: King, church and supermarkets

At school, as a kid, she had learned that Viborg City was one of the most democratic city-states of the entire Western Cities' Alliance. People envied it from all over the world, and it was often cited as a model in international conferences.

And that was why it now had to protect itself from the hordes of new immigrants from Samarqand and the never-ending flux of gypsies

coming from the Eastern Cities' Federation. Although a child of immigrants herself, Leila could understand perfectly well why the anti-immigrant laws had been passed. Her heart could disagree with the special NonCitizen cards they were given (Her parents had had a NewCit card for years, and that was okay too) and the general violence that was used against them, both symbolic and real, but her mind accepted it because it was the only thing the city could do to remain the democratic paradise that shone over all other cities.

Yet, here, in the middle of this paradise, she wished that one day, she could be part of it, and not just because of marriage or luck.

"We're almost there," Maria said.

This summed up perfectly Leila's feelings. And frustrations.

SIGRID.

Sigrid looked at the old map of Viborg City pinned on the wall of her office. The three main districts of the city were represented with different colors;light blue (for despair?) for Sorgbjerg, the NoCred area; green (for envy?) for the H.C. Andersen district, land of the Creds; and, strangely, pale red for Kong Kristian, the Cash paradise. Why red, she wondered, the color of socialism and revolutions? One of the discreet ironies of the system? A Pavlovian lie, to keep up appearances? It should have been white, she thought, like the nickname the citizens of Sorgbjerg had given it, and which had passed in everyday language: "White City", because all the villas were white and their owners too. There was a flag pinned right in the middle of it—the police station. The flag was a minuscule national flag. For God and country. And money. Especially money.

LEE JR.

Lee sat in the quiet café on the corner of Bergman and Hamsun with a warm and outrageously expensive *café latte* in front of him. It never ceased to amaze him how expensive things were here. And how bad service was. The young woman behind the bar had served him and taken his money without a smile or even a friendly look. New Babylon could be criticized for a lot of things—from its imperialistic politics to its shitty commercial culture which poisoned the entire world—but at least people, in general, were friendly, even when they were paid shitty wages. And here, they were actually paid *good* wages.

Oh no, he thought, *here I am—speaking like Lee Senior*.

He had chosen to sit by the large bay window, so he could watch the passers-by. His girlfriend wouldn't be back for a while, so he had the entire afternoon for himself. Sometimes, he could feel really lonely here. He missed his friends from Babylon, who were not many, but a good bunch of happy drinkers, both male and female. His best friends here were his computer and the notebook in which he scribbled ideas and references for his novels. Sometimes he thought about getting a cat for company. Then again, cats didn't talk much, if at all.

Lee opened his notebook and looked at what he had jotted down the past few days.

Nazi witch hunt.
Secret Nazi program.
Thule Society.
Vril Society.
Ahnenerbe.
Himmler.
Otto Rahn.
Mages vs Witches.
Main characters: young Gypsy woman, young German warlock, Jewish astrologuer, Nazi mages, Himmler, Otto Rahn, Maria Orsic.

And that was all for now. He didn't have a title either and Joe, his agent, had just asked for one. The book was due in a year. Another bestseller, he hoped. In New Babylon and New Petersburg, at least. Here, he would never make it. They probably didn't even know who Himmler was.

What Beauty Is.

Coloring hair
Coloring life.

Leila.

Stepping out of the car, Leila took a look around. White City, as it always was. Large white villas, mowed lawns, trees and hedges, beautiful cars, (most in closed garages). If Viborg City was known as the "Red City" across the world because of its red brick buildings, and as "Boring City" because all the buildings looked the same, Kong Kristian seemed to be an independent entity—which in fact, it almost was. Or *really* was.

Nothing in daily life seemed connected to it. It was almost never mentioned in the media; Kong Kristian (White City's official name) was rarely shown on television, apart from a few interviews like the one she was supposed to do today, and never referred to as social problem or question. It just hung there, in mid-air in the city's soul, like an invisible head. And then again, if someone or something severed that phantom head, the city would probably die. At least, that's the way she saw it. The way she was raised to see it, her boyfriend would have argued. But what did he know? He wasn't even from here. He knew nothing.

"Are we ready?" she said, watching Maria set the camera on her shoulder. It was a rhetorical question of course, and Maria didn't even answer. Leila connected the wireless microphone to the camera, waiting for the diode light to blink blue.

LEE JR.

Maybe he should have been a poet, Lee sometimes told himself. His father had once met the famous (or infamous, according to what side of Babylonian pre and post-war politics you belonged to) Al Alamein, the poet who had created a huge political incident between New Babylon and New Petersburg way back when, and had told his son how lucky (in his eyes) the guy had been: one poetry collection censored and fame had knocked at his door. Lee Jr. had objected that the poor man had been banned for life from Babylon, which seemed to be still painful for him— Lee had seen and read a couple of interviews of the poet where he apparently missed Babylon very much and hoped his sentence would be revised one day. Lee Sr. had chuckled: "Anybody can live with that amount of pain if it makes you regularly appear on TV." Lee Jr. sipped the last drops of his coffee and stood up to leave. Nope, he could never be a poet—not enough pain.

Dear Diary.

What do I remember before 1945? Joy. Joy and privations. A daily intoxication. The wait for something beautiful, more beautiful than I was living then. They had promised us beauty. I was waiting for it. Eager. And they were right. Beauty came and it was worth the wait.

SIGRID.

What can be explained? What cannot be explained? Can anything be explained at all? Does it matter, in the end? Mystery and questions, that's how people saw police work. But it wasn't really like that. It was more like: Violence and a poor explanation.

Motives were always disappointing. Greed. Jealousy. Bad craziness. All were generally simplistic.

Very disappointing, indeed.

On the other hand, she had *chosen* to become a cop and she did love her job. Most of the time. Or until now, at least.

She grabbed one of three files lying on her desk but didn't open it. Her mind was somewhere else, on how she had ended up in White City. The funniest thing was that she didn't regret a thing and she would do it again if she had to. In that sense, her punishment was a complete failure. She would never bow her head and ask for forgiveness. But here, there wasn't any chance anything like *that* would happen again.

Chosen to become a cop, yes. After her law studies. Her parents thought she was crazy. They were old socialists—though actually middle-of-the-road social democrats today—and thought it a disgrace to work for The Man or rather, if not truly a disgrace, at least incomprehensible. Both good Cred citizens—her father was a public hospital doctor, her mother a librarian—they still held a profound distrust for the police since the South-East China war and the death of peace activist Julie Bjerregard, who had been found murdered in her apartment. She had been the leader of the movement of protest against the Western Alliance, and close to the famous Potemkin Crew hacker group, who had managed to hack and sabotage military satellites.

Julie had also been a close friend of Diana, Sigrid's mother. The police had said that her boyfriend had murdered her while hallucinating on drugs and then committed suicide by jumping out of the 6th floor window of their apartment. The problem was that Diana knew the couple

very well and they never took drugs—they weren't even social smokers. Actually, they were quite the exception in the little activist group. So, since then, Sigrid's parents had suspected foul play from Viborg City police directly under the secret orders of New Babylon.

After her own episode, she admitted that her parents, alas, might have been right: there was definitely something rotten in the Viborg City police department. If not in the entire city itself.

Leila.

"So you've organized this Tax Defense League. Can you tell us a little bit more about what it's about?"

The old hag, with her 2000 crowns haircut, her Nordic-themed gold chain, her French nail varnish and lipstick, and her Italian silk blouse smiled at the camera. Her whitened teeth must have also cost a fortune.

"Well, you see, all of us here (She made a large gesture enveloping the surrounding villas), we have worked hard in order to live here. So when the government announced that the roofs would be taxed according to their surface, we thought that it was too much. We couldn't accept this."

Leila nodded mechanically at the other end of the microphone, thinking *What the fuck am I doing here?* Her ear caught the humming of a motorcycle in the background. She hoped it wouldn't fuck up the sound of the interview because she really didn't want to go through with it again.

"So what are you going to do with this association?"

"Well, we have contacted our local politicians, of course—my husband happens to be good friends with some of them . . . "

She paused and stared at Leila as if to make sure the little brown journalist understood the implications of that sentence. Leila boiled inside. She had no problems with the Viborg City class-division—Cash, Credit and No-Credit- but she did hate being reminded of it by the people who were in the superior layer.

The motorcycle droned closer and parked in the front of a villa down the street. In the corner of her eye, Leila saw the driver dismount and ring the bell. His helmet was still on. Must have been in a hurry.

"Anyway," the white-haired vampire resumed, "we are ready to take some drastic actions, like investing all our saving in foreign banks. And if that doesn't . . . "

Fireworks? Leila thought, startling at the short deflagration.

Instinctively turning her head, she saw the driver throw something

away on the front lawn and hop back onto his motorcycle. Two seconds later, he was gone. A strong smell of powder filled the air—which reminded her again of fireworks. Then she realized that the villa's door was still open and that they were two feet sticking out, motionless.

Oh my God! She thought, *Oh my God, Oh my God, Oh my God—a scoop!*

Dog Poem #2

All territories
Are invisible
Only violence
Makes them
Visible

LEE JR.

Back in the tiny apartment, Lee was surfing on the internet, gathering more data for his next novel. His little walking tour had unblocked some ideas and he had a better view on his project now. The title, even. His agent would be happy. *Hexen*. "Witch," in German. Perfect. He had to admit that the red bricks and the weird gothic style of Viborg City's dark streets did help his inspiration. A good thing they spoke Nordic and not German—he would have felt very claustrophobic.

The story itself was beginning to unfold nicely: Before the Second World War, the Nazis were also persecuting witches, using mages to find them. The heroine was a German girl with witch-like powers in Berlin in 1938. A blonde, blue-eyed Aryan witch, who was going to side with her Jewish and Gypsy kin in an underground resistance movement.

Viborg-City had just voted some very restrictive laws against gypsies and "nomadic immigrants." The synchronicity was uncanny. Of course, Lee had only read about it in the Babylonian electronic papers—so he couldn't get the whole story—but it did sound pretty harsh and scary. He had also read an article last week about some Old Delhi lecturer from Viborg City university who had been beaten up by cops during an identity check. They had thought he was a Gypsy and had apologized afterwards. The lecturer sued them, but his complaint was been dismissed because, precisely, the police made official apologies.

His mobile phone rang and he picked it up. His girlfriend would come home late today. No problem. He had some Nazis to take care of.

SIGRID.

A murder on the first day of her new job! And Jørgensen, her teammate, on sick leave . . . Probably the first interesting event in two decades in White City, and it fell on her shoulders because of bureaucratic hierarchy.

Talk about a coincidence!

Sigrid had seen the half-annoyed, half-frightened look in Møltke's eyes when he had told her she would be in charge. Annoyed, because he and she knew all the others would be jealous. Frightened, because he and she knew he had to give it to her, otherwise she could have filed a complaint against him for not respecting the rules. She knew that look well. She called it "The Viborg-City Look." She saw it flash many times during a day. The fear of doing something wrong while not certain of doing something right, and being caught in the act.

Sartre would have loved that look.

She was sitting on the passenger seat of an unmarked car now, looking out as they were cruising the streets of White City, humming to herself. She felt like in a movie with Marlene Dietrich, one of those noir Weimar Republic films announcing the darker days ahead. Except that the darker days were already here, but had been artificially colorized.

Leila.

Leila had immediately called Lene at the TV station. Her boss had said she was going to send a van with some live transmission gear. Leila hoped she would send the gear only, and not another reporter to replace her, although that was very likely. This was bound to make national headlines. The old lady was in shock and was now sitting on a chair, in her house, hyperventilating.

"Aren't you going to call the cops?" Maria asked.

"Wait," Leila said. "Come with me. This is our big chance."

"Chance for what?"

Leila sighed and didn't answer. *To make it into the national news department, you stupid fuck. To have your own show one day. To have all the powerful people of this city eat in the palm of your hand.*

She ran to the other house, dragging Maria behind her like a reluctant dog on a leash, with her mike still attached on the camera

"Wait! Wait! I can't run that fast"

"We're almost there!"

The man lay on his back, face turned to the left. His glasses had flown into the corridor. A huge dark stain bubbled up on his chest, turning the blue cloth of his shirt into a blackish red. It didn't look at all like the ketchup or false blood they used in the movies.

Leila kneeled beside him and felt his pulse. Nothing, and the skin was already losing its warmth.

"Okay, film this!" she commanded Maria. "Film this!"

She stood up and began speaking, staring at the camera and moving around to explain what had happened.

It was only when she heard the sirens wailing closer and closer that she realized she had completely forgotten to call the cops.

SIGRID.

Her driver was a uniformed young kid with a baby face. He had multiple spots of acne, as if he had been shot with a zit shotgun. He reminded her of a boyfriend she had in high-school. She had actually gone out with him because of his zits—she felt sorry for him. His eyes had been beautiful, though. Deep blue with silver specks.

The young cop's eyes didn't have that usual dead look yet—they still sparkled too much. He seemed nervous though, chewing on imaginary gum.

"First homicide?" she asked loudly, as the siren howled above.

He nodded, looking straight over the wheel.

"You'll see, it's fun," she joked.

She wondered if he would get it, or if he would file a complaint against her for her "inappropriate remark." *Probably none of the above. Too stupid and too young.* She sighed silently. *What was this city coming to? A murder in White City?* She smiled. *Actually, there might be hope, after all.*

Dear Diary.

To explain something unexplainable is faith. Its meaning can only come through faith. But a faith understood from birth—not something learned. That was the mistake the first time, the illusion. We believed faith could be given, could be taught. But no. Faith has to be invisible, fed from the start in fragments no one can notice, through television, radio, science, games, music, news—anything that both hides and conveys the message, without religion. Religion was the mistake, for it is anything but universal. It's personal. It's bound to fail. The message has to be invisible and has to be beautiful—it has to make you feel beautiful. Then you can become the monster. And you won't even realize it. Because the monster has become universal.

LEE JR.

The grayness of spring. He had never thought about that before moving to Viborg City. Spring in Babylon was a mixture of colors, sometimes dark, sometimes bright, but everything here was only different shades of grey. Once again, he had to admit it, it proved useful for his novel—he had visited Old Berlin and had been really disappointed by its modernity. A new city, a new place—all of its evil buried deep under parks, lakes, and artificial forests. He understood why—and the people there had been so helpful and friendly that he only had good memories of the city—but it had been disastrous for his inspiration. He had hoped to recapture some of the bad and evil craziness of the 30s, but no—nothing. Even the World War Two museum had been squeaky clean. His week had ended up in a drinking binge with his Berlin publisher and her friends— inspiration for another novel, maybe, but surely not this one. Lee's eyes moved from the window back to the computer screen. *Otto Rahn looked out of the car's window*, he typed. *It was a gray rainy day. So much for spring, Rahn thought. So much for spring.*

SIGRID.

The driver stopped the car right in front of the house. The two other police cars parked a little bit further down the street. A small group of frightened neighbors stood by, chatting and shaking heads.

There already was a local news van near the villa, which both surprised and annoyed Sigrid. *How could have they come so fast? Did the killer call them up? Why not a national channel then?* Questions, questions, questions. And she hadn't even gotten out of the car yet.

The TV crew was standing by the open door. At least, they were not filming, which meant they weren't on live. Good. Good. They looked stunned, which was understandable. There was a Samarqandi-looking young woman in long red coat, and a chubby short blonde, holding the camera in her arms, as if it was a sleeping baby or a small dog. The microphone hung loosely from the Samarqandi's hand, making her the reporter.

Ignoring them for now, the detective-inspector stood in front of the opened entrance door, looking down at the dead man lying on his back in a puddle of dark blood. Mid-fifties, white, glasses (they had fallen from his face—she had almost trodden on them while approaching the front door), nice clothes (of course), single or his family was away. Three bullets in the chest (one in the heart—lucky shot, probably, as the two other ones stood far apart). Didn't look professional—no bullet in the head to make sure the job was done.

Sigrid told the cops coming out of the other cars to set-up a secured perimeter around the house and turned to the TV crew standing on the wet lawn by the open door. She opened her wallet to show her legitimation. The journalist and the camera girl both nodded silently.

"When did you arrive? Did you see anything?"

"Yes. Well, no, not really. But we heard everything. And I saw the guy—murderer, killer, whatever. From the corner of my eye. A motorbike. We were interviewing a lady. She is inside now. I mean, in her own house. There."

The Samarqandi-looking girl had spoken. Perfect Nordic accent. Probably born here. Lucky for her. Good speech was the only way up, in this city. You could be a genius, but if you had the wrong skin color and wrong accent, nobody would hire you. Nobody. Not even your local supermarket. Unless you were 17 and could be paid below the minimum wage. *Open society, my ass.*

"Did you film anything?"

"Yes. No. Well, him," the reporter said, pointing at the body. "But not the killer, no."

Sigrid asked the TV more questions, but didn't get much info: a black motorcycle, make unknown, with a rider dressed in black, and that was it. The reporter pointed at the gun lying in the grass, which Sigrid hadn't noticed. Looked like a 9mm from here.

She thanked the reporters, asked a cop in uniform to write down their names and telephone numbers.

"Can I have your phone number too? Or your email?" the reporter asked. "I would like to follow up on this . . . "

Sigrid grimaced inside, although her face didn't move an inch. She knew that meant daily phone calls and emails—but she couldn't say no. She couldn't afford more bad publicity if she wanted to "follow up" on this case herself, so she typed down her info on the extended smartphone, making a single typo on the email and inverting two numbers on her phone number.

"Thank you" the reporter said.

"You're welcome," Sigrid answered, flashing her most diplomatic smile.

What Beauty Is.

Yes.
Polished face.

Leila.

Leila observed the inspector talk to the other cops. "Sigrid Wulff," she had typed. Probably one of the most stunningly beautiful woman she had seen in her life. Venetian blonde hair, blue eyes so pale they almost looked translucent, darker sharp high-brows, long face with a nice square jaw, medium-sized mouth with full lips—she really looked like one of those old glamorous film stars of the 30s. Striking. And professional, too. She handled those boys with an iron hand.

"Here they come," Maria said. "I guess we're finished here."

Leila felt her heart sink underneath her red wool coat. A national channel VCTV 2 News van had parked right next to theirs. And, of course, who else but Jan Nilsson to jump out of the passenger's seat? She saw him scan the area, his icy blue eyes trying to find her so she could give him a full briefing. *Fuck that shit*, she thought. *I was here first.* He spotted her and began to jog her way. Maria began to wave, but Leila dragged her along with the mike's chord.

"What are you . . . ?"

"Shut up. We were here first. Local is going to be faster than national, for once."

She hurried past a flabbergasted Jan, hopped in the car and had Maria drive away as fast as she could. In the rear-view mirror, she saw Jan lift his hands up in the air and shake his head. And that felt GOOD.

2. DOCTOR PRESCRIBES HEALTHCARE COST SAVINGS PLANS TO GOVERNORS

SIGRID.

Sigrid looked at her computer screen, mentally summing-up the info of the last two days. She could actually have watched the TV instead, as the murder had been the hottest "Breaking News" topic in the last 48 hours.

The victim was Niels Kepler, known in the media as "White Power Niels," little brother to Marta Kepler, the heir and CEO of Phoebus Cosmetics, the famous beauty products corporation, a heavyweight in international trade. Niels sat at the board, but had no real power—his shares gave him substantial monthly revenue, but not a majority. Marta reigned as an absolute monarch. An invisible one too, as she never appeared in public. She was a recluse in her White City mansion, located a few streets away from her brother's villa.

Niels Kepler had also caused some commotion recently, by asking for the complete outlawing of Gypsies in Viborg City. A following poll had shown that a majority of the VC population "agreed totally" or "somewhat agreed" with him, and while the Liberal-Conservative government had officially denounced Kepler's rant, they had still added a few paragraphs to the already restraining laws, causing a brief international incident with the rest of the Western Alliance cities, who strongly "disapproved" of the measures. Sigrid knew there was also a large approval of Kepler in the police force—her "incident" had been proof of that, had she needed any.

Kepler openly supported the small National Liberal Identity Party, who was part of the government's right-wing coalition. He also funded them, along with other large corporations, who saw them as "friendly" to their investments and lack of morals.

Sigrid sipped some cold coffee from her plastic cup. She was actually really glad somebody had popped the fucker. But, of course, she was going to keep that thought to herself—although she *had* told her cat.

LEE JR.

Leila had been in a terrible mood in the past week, and he could understand why. To be taken off a scoop you had been a witness to and the first to announce was like a huge slap in the face.

The whole thing had exploded like a bag of dog poop held by a two year old tripping on a concrete sidewalk. Even with his limited Nordic, he could see the shockwave of the murder in the newspaper headlines, in the news; he recognized the name on the radio. The murder seemed to have caused an earthquake in a country completely without fault-lines.

But Leila was a fighter, he knew it. She had told him she had confronted her boss and filed a complaint to the higher-ups—although, in his opinion, the higher-ups were directly responsible for this, but he kept it to himself—no need to destroy his girlfriend's illusions.

She left for her job every morning with a closed face and felt sorry for her. At the same time, her attitude fueled the main character in his novel, a fighter too. He had finally found her name after watching an interview with the inspector in charge of the case—a stunning blonde with the palest blue eyes: Sigrid Wulf (he had taken out an "f" for legal reasons.) She would make the perfect heroine. Someone to die for. And many would, for sure.

Dog Poem #3

Animal art
Is pure
Animal art
is violence
Animal art
Is merciless

Leila.

Could she be actually experiencing some kind of a nervous breakdown? It was the first time she had felt so much like shit. She couldn't see Lene without feeling like smashing her pretty professional face into bloody chunks of flesh and bone. Maybe with a hammer. Or a heavy ashtray. In any case, the thought made her feel good. Actually, it was the only thing that made her feel good.

How could that bitch have accepted to take her out of the Kepler murder? She had been there first! She had offered the local channel a "Breaking News" report! That was the first time in the entire Viborg City media history that it had happened! And Lene, that fucking traitor, had given it all away to the national assholes, so Jan Nilsson could run away with all the credit. Leila felt tears of rage burn the corner of her eyes.

She tried to focus on her notes for the interview she had scheduled in the afternoon. A baby crocodile had been born at the zoo. She hoped a commercial airliner would crash on it during her interview with the zoo-keeper so she would get a second chance.

SIGRID.

Terror! Terror! Everything was "Terror," and she was getting sick of it. The media had cranked the "terror" volume to the max, interfering directly with her investigation. Of course, it was all because of domestic politics—the governing coalition needed the National Liberal Identity Party's votes on almost everything, and those bastards were using this to their bastardly advantage. The upcoming election in six months wasn't helping any, either.

Sigrid hadn't voted in the last ten years, a rational choice in her eyes. Why vote for a system that only worked for its elite? Viborg City prided itself in being one of the best democracies in the world, when it was in fact completely corrupt from the inside. Sure, they had a proportionally elected assembly, with a threshold as low as 2 percent. Sure, there were a multiplicity of parties. But only three newspapers, two of them owned by the same trust fund. The third was owned by another trust fund, that also owned two of the four TV channels. There was one state radio station, and a constellation of commercial ones, all basically playing the same music. The trade unions were all yellow, working hand in hand with the large corporations.

Sure, you could see penises and trimmed bushes on TV, swear-words weren't replaced by ludicrous cartoon sounds as in New Babylon, you could make racist jokes on the radio, draw xenophobic caricatures—but that was the gloss over the grim truth. She felt she lived in a totalitarian user-friendly state, and nothing around her challenged her perception. Quite the contrary.

As to prove her point even more, she had been assigned a secret service supervisor, who called her basically every day to ask her what she had found, and who in return gave her nothing. He insisted on having someone from his service be present at all her interrogations. Waste of public money, waste of time.

Sigrid felt that this murder had nothing to do with "terror." The weapon was old and had probably been sold to someone who didn't

know anything about them. The killer had been lucky it hadn't exploded in his or her hand, and Kepler unlucky because it hadn't jammed. The shots had been fired point blank, yet they were far apart. She had told Møltke about her doubts, but he had shrugged and said: "Keep looking where you are asked to look."

So here she was, in some poor Gypsy association's local, interrogating five frightened young men, escorted by twelve officers in full anti-terror uniform, only because someone had called her to give her a "tip" she knew wouldn't lead to anything, but had to follow up anyway.

Dear Diary.

Before the war, there was struggle. We were a minority, only carried by our love of beauty. We were laughed at, shunned, attacked. But we shone through and we temporarily won. It was the victory of pure beauty. And it was even more beautiful because it was temporary. Our ruins became our foundations.

LEE JR.

Lee stretched on his chair and shut down his computer. It had been a good day of research and writing. Sigrid Wulf was taking shape, a young beautiful Aryan witch who wasn't aware of her powers yet in 1938 Germany.

He needed to go out now and meet people. It was still early in the afternoon, and coffee was calling. He decided to go to the only good bookstore he knew in Viborg City—i.e. with real books instead of those supermarkets filled with download machines. It was called The Forgotten Shelf and was owned by Carlo, who looked like a dark Jewish Emile Zola. Carlo sold second and third-hand books, along with some rare first editions. It was a little dark shop, with colorful paperback walls and a spicy scent of dust, located in the NoCred part of Viborg City, Sorgbjerg, which was also, not surprisingly, the most lively.

Lee loved to go there and chat with Carlo—who had actually read his books and enjoyed them—or so he politely said. That is where he had met his only true friend so far in this city, Tarek Khan, a Samarqandi writer and journalist who had come to Viborg City ten years ago to study and had decided to stay because he had met Astrid, whom he had married.

Tarek worked free-lance for various papers—who published him when he criticized Samarqand's politics and didn't publish him when he didn't—and, like Lee, he was well-known everywhere else. His novels had been translated in various languages, and Lee knew who he was before he had actually met him, although he hadn't—at the time—read any of his books.

Lee hoped he would be there—he often came to the store to buy books in English and chat with Carlo. It would be a good change from those Nazis he was writing about.

Leila.

Leila knocked on the door of their small flat, but no one answered. She took out her keys and let herself in. Lee wasn't home. It wasn't the first time, but it was a rare occurrence. *Too rare, actually*, she thought. *The boy is living in his own prison.* She hung her jacket and checked her phone. There was a message. He was with Tarek and would be coming back late. Good for him. He needed to make this city his home at some point.

When she had met him in New Babylon, she had seen him as an independent, wild, intense young man. A published and famous genre writer, he was always going out to parties, meeting old and new friends in bars and cafés, out to sign books in various bookstores. She was afraid sometimes that bringing him back here wasn't so great an idea.

While she was studying Journalism and Media at New Babylon University, Viborg City had appeared to her as a sort of perfect paradise compared to the harsh conditions one sometimes could be confronted with in New Babylon. Now she wasn't so sure anymore. Lee had been very critical since his arrival, and although it hurt her deeply—more deeply than she wanted to admit—she couldn't blame it only on his poor master of the Nordic language.

She turned on the TV with the remote and went into the kitchen to fix herself some dinner.

Not everything was perfect in Viborg City. The "Gypsy laws," for one. She wasn't sure about them. Sure, something had to be done to protect the city against all those illegal immigrants, especially if you wanted to protect the social system—but to witness how violently this was done made her wince sometimes. But to Lee, this was like Nazi Germany and he could not discuss it with her without getting upset. So they had stopped discussing politics.

The fridge was almost empty, so she opened the freezer and took a pizza out. She wasn't that hungry anyway. Her anger killed any appetite in her. That was another problem she could see in Viborg City: injustice,

and the fact that nobody ever complained. Ever. She had gone to see her union representative this morning, and he had told her that she should withdraw her complaint and apologize to Lene, because Lene had only done what she had felt right for the company. What? *What?*

Leila felt a wave of quicksilver adrenaline shoot up her spine. Her hands were trembling with anger as she unwrapped the pizza and put it in the oven. Lee had told her she should fight back, until they would get tired of it and put her back on this case. Now she could see it would lead her nowhere, except maybe getting fired.

Sighing, she took a half-full bottle of red wine and sat in front of the TV in the dining room.

As to deliberately make things worse, she saw her story on the baby crocodile at the zoo. She recalled the stench and the humid warmth of the reptile section. She grimaced and took a sip of her wine. When Lee would come back, he would find a drunk girlfriend willing to do *anything* to stop procrastinating. Specifically about Lene and crocodiles.

What Beauty Is.

He thinks I'm a natural
I love the feel of it

SIGRID.

She badly needed a drink. She needed to forget all about this impossible case for a while and enjoy life just a little bit. There was a bar at the corner of her street where she felt comfortable. They made superb cocktails. They had one with the perfect name: Marlene Dietrich. It was champagne-based and she had decided it was her favorite.

Combing her hair, Sigrid looked at herself in the mirror. How long since she had a real good night of sex? It wasn't that difficult to calculate actually—that was the last time she had sex, during her summer holiday last year, in New Paris, with a beautiful stranger she had met at a museum. A perfect start for a romantic movie, although it had ended with her fleeing from the hotel room at five in the morning, before he woke up. Romance scared her shitless But she did enjoy being physical. Not the same thing—at all. Contrary to love, when you fucked, you could still have your armor on.

THEORY OF POWER #2

What you can't force onto people, sell it to them.
They will always buy it.

LEE JR.

In the bus taking him home, Lee realized that he was quite drunk. Tarek had been in a good mood and had bought a lot of rounds. Carlo had joined them after closing down his shop, quiet and mysterious as usual, but also warm and friendly.

It had started as a wonderful literary afternoon. Lee had found Tarek already chatting with Carlo, sitting in one of the two old armchairs standing next to the book-covered counter. Tarek and Carlo were drinking some mocha that the bookstore owner cooked in the shop's little kitchen, spreading around a marvelous smell. Later, Tarek had decided to go buy some beers and the day had tilted towards a less literary, but funnier atmosphere. They had a quick kebab at the local Samarqandi fast-food, then hurried to a bar, where they kept on drinking, celebrating Tarek's new novel's international success. They toasted to the Viborg City literary critics that had not written a single line about it, and to all the others in the other major cities who had.

"It's funny," Tarek said at some point, "but in my eyes, Viborg City is the most expensive open prison in the world."

The sentence still rang in Lee's head, going round and round like a dark shiny mantra.

SIGRID.

She was being fucked by a complete moron and she was loving it. He had a gorgeous body and no brains—a bank clerk, if she remembered correctly. Or a real-estate agent. Whatever. The champagne bubbles in her stomach tickled her from the inside as he rammed her pink moist treasure-chest. Exactly what she needed. Once in a while, life offered some soothing balm to rub upon your third-degree burns. And you had to press the tube until the last drop, because who knew if there would be any left in stock tomorrow?

LEE JR.

Lee fell, panting, over Leila's warm and welcoming body. He lay for a few seconds upon her, her hand stroking his back. When the pleasure sparkles finally vanished from his mind, he suddenly realized he had spent the whole day without thinking once about his father.

Leila.

"What are you doing? Who is that?"

Leila turned around. Lee was standing behind her in his underwear. She was sitting on the couch of their small dining room, her laptop opened on the table.

"You want some coffee?," he asked.

She shook her head "no".

"Who's that?" Lee asked again, pointing at the photos displayed on her screen.

"That's Niels Kepler. The victim. And that's his sister, Marta, the CEO of Phoebus Cosmetics."

Lee bent over to take a closer look.

"Wow! She's a looker!"

"This picture was taken in the 80s," Leila replied sourly. "It's actually the only picture we have of her."

"Why? She died too?"

"No. She is just very reclusive. And in Viborg City, contrary to Babylon, we respect famous peoples' private lives."

"So, no coffee?"

"No."

Shaking his head, Lee disappeared in the tiny kitchen.

Leila stared at Marta Kepler's photo. She might have found her revenge and her way to the top at the same time. Lene would cry her eyes out if this worked out. *You clever girl*, Leila mouthed to herself. *Clever, clever girl.*

Dear Diary.

Arcades and colonnades. A smell of Europe: gas and jasmine. The purity of strength, the beauty of contained violence. We were wanting, we were eager. The old runes helped us see the hole beneath the Earth. Our past. Our glorious past. The Old Race we had forgotten, but stumbled upon through an accident of history. In the twenties, there was darkness and perfume. My father, working with his magical smells. I remember: kissing his cheek and feeling happy because of the whiff of his cologne. A mosaic of memories—I was sixteen then. And since then I am sixteen forever. Beautiful forever. Inside.

3. WHAT KIND OF VEGETARIAN WAS HITLER?

SIGRID.

So the killer was a white male. She felt like laughing out loud, even if it wasn't funny, but Møltke had just left her office and she was afraid he might hear her. He had rushed in with the DNA results, avoiding her eyes as he told her the conclusions of the laboratory. Now he would have to contact the press, and some people would be very unhappy. She couldn't wait to see the face of the National Liberal Identity Party leader later today. Sigrid looked at the paper again. White male. And it came directly from the gun. Impossible to deny. She knew what she had to do now: go back to all these immigrant centers and apologize. Personally.

Dog Poem #5

Growl, bark and bite
Foam at the mouth
Pure beauty
of rage
And strength

Leila.

She had gotten back into her pre-murder routine, like everybody else. There hadn't been anything new on the case since it was revealed that the murderer presumably was a white male, and that had been announced two weeks ago. Now the police said they were focusing on extreme-left terrorists, which made sense. Everything was back to normal—except she still wanted her revenge on Lene and Jan Nilsson, those fuckers. And she would get it. She was actually working on it, like termites worked on the foundations of a house, until everything collapsed.

LEE JR.

Lee took a sip of his now cold coffee and put the cup down next to his laptop. The development of the novel was going well, but he needed to do more research on the Nazi occult link. So far, he had worked with general books about Nazi occultism, but he felt he still lacked something darker or crazier, if possible.

He had Otto Rahn, the *Anherebe*, the Thule Society, Himmler, etc. It was all good for background construction, but he wanted something both historical and weird in a non-Gothic way. He wanted fiction within fiction. After all, the whole Nazi thought was based on pure, dangerous fiction, from crazy archeology to non-existing blood types. Lee wanted something that would show this, beyond the mere "horror story" he was writing. Something his readers would look up because they wanted to know if he had invented it or not, the secret pleasure of all writers added to the feeling he had touched something real.

He looked at his phone and hesitated. It would be a first, and he wasn't sure it would go well. But maybe, *he* would know. He always did. Sighing, he dialed the number and waited.

"Dad, it's me . . . Yeah, good, good—everything's fine, don't worry . . . No, I called you because I thought you might be able to help me with my new novel . . . No, not the one that just came out, the one I'm working on now . . . Yes . . . "

SIGRID.

The young woman in charge of the immigrants' shelter stood up as Sigrid walked in, looking frightened. The three Gypsy youths sitting at the little round table in the foyer stopped in the middle of their card game. Sigrid saw their jaws clench and the deep frown on their foreheads. They all remembered her, and the ten policemen that had escorted her last week. This was the first shelter she had decided to visit. There were ten in the city in all. It wasn't going to be easy, but she knew she owed it to them. And to her city too, strangely enough. To the good old warm city VC had once been, a symbol of tolerance and democracy. Once upon a time. Yes. Exactly. Once upon a time. She smiled, but nobody smiled back.

What Beauty Is.

Oh, silly curls!
Oh, pout!
Oh, rapture!

Leila.

Leila re-read the paragraph from the Wikipedia article on Phoebus Cosmetics for the second time. There must have been a mistake: It said that Phoebus industries had been founded by Hans Kepler in 1949 in Viborg City, who had emigrated there after the war with his two children, Marta and Niels. Their mother had died during an Allied bombing. Nothing more. But it was impossible: Niels Kepler was said to be 43 years old and Marta was supposedly two years older. Marta and Niels couldn't have come with their parents in 1949! They would have been at least in their late seventies today!

Cursing the online Encyclopedia, she typed in more words to refine her search. After ten minutes, she gave up. There was nothing else—nothing on the birth dates of both Marta and Niels, and no pictures of their childhood. Only that one and only picture of Marta, taken supposedly fifteen years ago—and where she looked twenty. Because of his political ideas, there were a lot more pictures of Niels, but the earliest dated back some ten years ago. Leila decided to check on the father, see if there was anything interesting on the Net about him. And there was. So much that her eyes opened wide and her lips mouthed a silent "Oh!"

SIGRID.

Sitting behind the wheel of her car, Sigrid took a deep breath and massaged her temples. She had just come out of the last immigrant center and had apologized personally to all those poor people she had terrorized the past weeks. Some had smiled, others had remained impenetrable—but all had wary eyes. The same eyes as prison mates have, and yet they were still free. Officially, at least.

She started the car and the noise of the engine momentarily replaced their faces. She felt tired, empty and angry. She felt like a bad cop. She felt like the Gestapo. Hell, she even *looked* like the Gestapo.

LEE JR.

Walking into Carlo's bookshop, Lee remembered the conversation he just had with his father. It had proved very useful, for once. He hadn't expected Lee senior to have known so much about crazy Nazi occult shit.

Apparently his father had wanted to write a novel about the subject himself, at some point of his life. Funny (or maybe just ironic) to think that father and son would meet through a common interest for the darkest aspect of humanity. Then again, that's what Lee senior's avant-garde novels had become famous for, and Lee Jr. wrote bestselling horror books—maybe not so surprising, after all.

Carlo greeted Lee in the empty shop. A timid sun flirted with the book covers, too weak to flip through the pages. Dusty smell of spring.

"Do you have anything about Nazi occultism?" Lee asked.

Carlo raised an eyebrow.

"Want to try something new?" he asked, caressing his beard. "Start the Fourth Reich?"

The young writer shook his head, smiling.

"Nothing like that. New book research."

"Nazis always sell well," Carlo said, pointing at a shelf in the back of the shop. "They help me pay the rent. My own little revenge."

THEORY OF POWER #3

To lie is a moral weakness, because one is afraid.

To hide the truth is not a weakness, because it comes from knowledge.

It is a necessity, as the truth is always blinding and it can hurt those who are not strong enough to understand.

Our enemies lie, we protect our loved ones.

We protect our people.

We protect our race.

Leila.

Leila heard the door open and Lee came in, holding a large plastic bag full of books. The evening was falling, turning the small apartment's windows a deep translucent blue. Spring was on its way. Soon the birds would start singing again at four in the morning. She loved that moment, when you could feel the seasons turn and churn. She stretched in front of her laptop as Lee put the bag down on their round dinner table.

"Carlo is great," he said. "I almost bought everything he had."

"I can see that," Leila answered, smiling. "What did you get?"

Lee began taking the books out. She frowned when she saw the swastikas and the SS emblems on the covers.

"Don't worry," Lee said. "I'm not turning into a Nazi. Just doing some research for my book."

Leila grabbed one of the books. *Hitler's Secret Space Program.*

"Funny," she said. "I'm also working with the Nazis. Well, sort of."

"Really?"

Leila nodded as Lee walked behind her chair. He bent over her shoulder to look at her screen, and she felt his cold hands slip into the collar of her t-shirt and grab her breasts. They instantly turned hard, although she didn't really want them to. He massaged them softly, grazing her nipples with his thumbs.

"You're looking at pictures of Hitler getting a haircut?"

"No, I'm looking at the guy cutting Hitler's hair."

She felt her breath run short, but managed to focus.

"That's Hans Kepler, Hitler's personal barber and perfumer," she resumed. "Marta and Niels Kepler's father."

Lee stopped caressing her for a second.

"What? But the pictures you showed me . . . He looked in his forties. And she—in her twenties? In the 80s? Did he have them late? Like . . . very late?"

"No, he came to Viborg City with them. But no birth dates are available. Very strange."

Lee began to nibble her ear, sending waves of wet electricity across her body.

"Maybe you should write my horror book," he whispered.

"Yes, maybe I should." She grinned.

"Let's fuck," he said.

"Yes. Let's."

Dog Poem #5

We take what we want
And we want everything

Sigrid.

There was a letter in her mailbox. From her trade union. She picked it up and opened the door of her flat. More good news probably. She dropped her jacket on a chair and went in the bathroom to start a bath. She needed to relax after the hard day. Of course, it was all her fault— she didn't really need to apologize to all those people, and if Møltke learned about that, he would probably have her fired immediately.

Speaking of which, she remembered the letter she was still holding. She opened it and frowned. The union was dropping her because of the incident. Stunned, she sat down and re-read the official dry prose. They said that she had acted unprofessionally, and that her attitude had "distressed" her colleagues.

The whole scene came back to her as a bad movie—her driving home at night, witnessing an identity control—one young gypsy-looking man surrounded by four uniformed cops, their two cars' revolving lights flashing like a crazy carousel—her stopping to see what was going on— the racist insults—the big cop punching the young man—twice—the other cops laughing—another punch—her getting out of the car—flashing her badge and screaming—the cops telling her not get involved—her asking their names- the young man not knowing what to do, her reaching out and grabbing his arm—telling him to get into her car—the cops sneering—her writing down their names from their uniform tags and leaving—leaving and watching the cops making obscene gestures in the rear mirror . . .

She had dropped the young man at his shelter—hadn't asked his name, which she regretted afterwards—and had driven home to write a report, which she had sent to the higher-ups—and which had resulted in her transfer to White City—and now this.

Racist government, corrupt media, yellow unions—well, she did need that hot bath more than ever. Maybe to drown herself.

Dear Diary.

The first experiments took place at Karl's place—I remember him so well—refined, virile, an elderly man in full mustache splendor—we sat at the table—Sigrun and I—she was 16, like me—and we heard them immediately—powerful voices from below—voices of truth and beauty—they spoke through us—they wrote through us—the Runes of the earth—the Runes of steel—the Runes of beauty—yes, this was in 1936, I remember everything—since that day, I have never forgotten a single thing—not one, not even half of one—I remember everything because I will need it all when they come back—bringing Sigrun and eternal beauty here, forever.

Leila.

She could hear Lee fix the dinner in the kitchen. Smells of vegetables and soy sauce ebbed their delicious way to her nostrils. She was still in bed, a sheet covering her thighs. The whole room smelled of sex. *Nazi sex.* She smiled for herself, feeling a little guilty. *One should not joke about these things.* Yet there was some truth in this. They had made really good love, and her skin still prickled with lazy pleasure. In a few minutes, he would call her from the kitchen. In a few minutes, the world would fall back in its precise position. "In a few minutes" felt like a wonderful stretch of eternity. *Great Nazi sex.* The words came back in her mind. A moment in time. Lee had to research his book, she had to find an angle in order to fuck that bitch Lene and beat Jan Nilsson to the top. Wasn't "fair competition" what society was all about, after all ? Since the fall of the Third Reich, at least?

"Dinner's ready!"

The world fell back into place. It was time to get up and move on. Move on and on.

4. STUDY TIES TROUBLED SLEEP TO LOWER BRAIN VOLUME.

SIGRID.

"Allô? Kepler Residence."

The woman's voice was old and cranky, as if worn out by centuries of suffering.

"Allô? Yes. I am Inspector Sigrid Wulff, of the Viborg City police department. I would like to speak to miss Kepler."

"I will ask if it's possible."

"Of course, it's possible. I am from the police department!"

"You have to call again tomorrow. I have to ask. Miss Kepler doesn't give interviews."

"It's not for an interview—I have to ask her some things about her brother."

"Then it *is* an interview. You can also send her questions by email, if you want."

"No, I need to see her. She has to speak to me."

"Call back tomorrow. I will ask."

Leila.

"Allô? Kepler residence."

The woman's voice was old and cranky, as if worn out by centuries of suffering.

"Allô? Yes. My name is Leila Bogossian. I am a journalist and I would like to interview miss Kepler."

"Miss Kepler doesn't give interviews."

"But it's not about her. I want to write a biography of her father."

"No interview. But you can send an email, if you want."

"Can you ask her?"

"No, I cannot. Send an email. Here is the address."

"Will she read my email?"

"Eventually"

Leila noted the address.

"Thank you."

The phone went dead. Leila looked at the email address. It was a long shot, but it was her best shot. She opened her laptop.

Dog Poem # 6

Bone
Is
Power
Power
Is
Bone

LEE JR.

Now, that was amazing. Incredible. Impossible. He had to show Leila, but she was at work and wouldn't be home until late, as usual. He almost felt like calling her, but he knew she wouldn't answer her phone. He had checked the Net, and had found the same picture. The one and only picture there was. But it was just . . . incredible.

SIGRID.

Her favorite bar. Again. Alone. Again. The waiter, a wonderful gay man in his early forties who allied humor, charm, and cocktail expertise, had some friends over and was chatting with them across the counter. On the television jutting from the wall at the other end, she could see the new suspects the media were pointing at Kepler's murder. This time it was the "Leftist" groups that were targeted—although the police had no actual leads. She knew. Hell, she *was* the police.

She took her sip of her Marlene Dietrich cocktail. Perfect, as usual. The bar was completely empty, apart for the happy group yapping with Henry, the bartender.

She felt like a cigarette. Of course, she always wanted what she couldn't have. Cigarettes. Lovers. Justice.

The TV showed a group of cops storming a squatters' building in Sorgbjerg. Close-ups of young kids with dyed black hair, piercings and hoodies. The "Breaking News" ribbon claimed that the police had received a new tip. Sigrid shrugged and lifted her glass again. *Bullshit.* Fortunately, there was always champagne.

Leila.

Lee seemed very happy and excited to see her, which was good because she had had a really shitty day at work. Lene had sent her to interview an idiot who grew roses in his garden. "The first roses of spring." How exciting. And she hadn't received any answer to her query about an interview with Marta Kepler. Yeah, if ever.

"You have to see this!" Lee said, not even kissing her, or waiting for her to take off her coat. "You won't believe it!"

Leila reluctantly followed him to the dining table, dragging her feet. Images of roses still whirled in front of her eyes. She would never buy flowers again.

"Look!"

Leila stared at the laptop's screen.

"What?" she asked, in a tired voice. "You found another picture of Marta Kepler. So what?"

Lee grinned.

"Look at the name. And date."

Leila squinted.

"Maria Sizic. 1938. What? Wait a minute . . . "

Lee grabbed her arm in his excitement.

"Isn't this incredible? This can't be just a coincidence, right?"

Leila was stunned. Lee was right. This person really looked like Marta Kepler. The picture was even taken at almost the same angle. But, of course, this was impossible.

"And I found more, " Lee said, dramatically. "It's all because of this new novel I'm working on—a secret war on witches during the Third Reich. I got interested in the Nazi occult societies, and fell on this picture. She was a member of The Black Sun Society. And guess who was too?"

Leila shook her head.

"I don't know? Hitler?"

"No. Better than that: Hans Kepler."

Leila felt her knees grow weak and she had to sit down.

"That wasn't in his official biography on Wikipedia," she said. "I haven't read about that anywhere."

"It's only mentioned in one book," Lee said. "And it's only in passing, in one paragraph. Wait . . . "

Lee grabbed a book from the pile that towered next to the laptop. He looked for a page and began reading: "The Black Sun Society comprised a diversity of members, ranging from the *Reichsführer* of the SS Heinrich Himmler to Hitler's barber and perfumer, Hans Kepler."

Leila's mind began to whirl. If she could get her interview, she could really, really blow Lene and Jan to smithereens. She just had to be careful not to get blown herself in the process.

What Beauty Is.

To him
You're just as lovely
As a movie star

5. TOP 10 HEALTHIEST CITIES IN THE WORLD.

SIGRID.

In the unmarked police car, Sigrid meditated on the expression "from bad to worse." Perfect definition of her present situation this morning.

Sitting behind the wheel next to her, Jørgensen was telling her his own opinion on how to deal with the "foreign scum" and the "crypto-bosheviks" who were "plaguing" this city. He had come back early from his paternal leave, to "help her", as he saw that the investigation was "going nowhere."

"Have you thought about a conspiracy between foreign elements and anarchist groups?" he asked her, shooting her an inquisitive side-glance. "They could be working together, with the support of Samarqand . . . "

Sigrid shrugged and looked out of the window.

"I think you watch too much TV," she said. "They're talking from the top of their heads. We have no serious leads. You know that. Just some DNA, which is from an unregistered white male. Who could be anybody."

Jørgensen grimaced.

"Most of the Lefties are white. But you know that, of course."

Sigrid couldn't tell how she should interpret that. Did Jørgensen know anything about the incident? Did he have access to her personal file? Or was it just a statement? The man was hard to read. Long and thin with a narrow reptilian face, steel blue eyes shining flatly through rimless glasses, he looked more like an evil banker than a cop.

"Here we are," he said, pulling in front of the local news channel.

She had to give an interview with one of the journalists there, about the Kepler murder. Møltke had ordered her to go instead of him, because it was on the local news. Nothing important, then. She sighed and got out of the car. Now it was "from worse to worse."

THEORY OF POWER #4

Everything is fragile. Everything can break. Even the heaviest hammer can break. But its strength lies in its ignorance of its own fragility.

LEE JR.

The waitress came and picked up their empty plates. Tarek dropped one sugar in his coffee, and thanked her. He winked at Lee as she made her way back to the café's kitchen.

"She's new. Very pretty, huh? They always have beautiful waitresses here. That's why I come all the time. And the food is not bad, for the price."

Lee nodded. Both statements were true.

"I'm going to New Petersburg next week," Tarek said.

"Hey, my hometown . . . "

"I know. I thought you might know some good places. Or your father."

Lee shook his head.

"Haven't been there in years. I moved to Babylon as soon as I graduated from high school. I'm sure the city's changed a lot since then. And Dad doesn't go out anymore. At least, I don't think so. Prefers to drink at home."

Remembering that his father had sounded sober on the last few phone calls, a pang of guilt flashed, warming Lee's ears.

"He used to, at least."

"Do you think there is any chance I could meet him? I would love to. Such a legend."

Lee senior's reputation was that of a mean recluse. Lee knew that his dad actually saw a lot of his friends, but none of them were journalists, reviewers, or had anything to do with the media. Hence the rep.

"Sure. You will just have to sign an agreement not to publish any of your conversations anywhere. I know it's weird, but all of his friends have signed it. Actually, I had to sign it too. I will call him and he will email me the form. I will forward it, you can print it, sign it and give it back to me. I will send it to him."

Tarek smiled.

"Sure. I love his novels. I would sign anything to get to see him. And I'm sure he will be happy to hear about his son."

Lee didn't know if that would matter so much to the old man, but he didn't want to let his bitterness shine through.

"Maybe, yeah. Say hi for me, in any case."

Tarek looked uneasy all of a sudden, as if something was bothering him.

"I have to tell you . . . I'm leaving Viborg City soon. That trip to New Petersburg is for a job. I've just been offered a position at their university. Apparently, some people do read my books, outside of this city. What's more—but this is still a secret—they might make a movie out of my last novel."

"Wow, man, that's great! Congratulations!"

Tarek turned his spoon in his coffee, like a witch making a nasty brew.

"I feel sorry leaving you here, all alone."

Lee laughed, but felt its hollowness.

"Don't worry, amigo. I'll survive."

"Perfect word, I'm afraid."

Lee waved at the waitress.

"Shall we have a cognac and celebrate?"

"Sure."

The waitress took the order with the impassibility suiting a goddess of beauty.

"Are you sure you want to stay here?" Tarek asked. "I know we've discussed this before. Leila's job, etc. But still—this is becoming more and more unbearable. All this xenophobic atmosphere . . . "

Lee sighed.

"I don't know. In a weird way, it inspires me. Everything here is so . . . alien, in a way. Like a time-warp. Monarchy, xenophoby, hard-line capitalism . . . Sometimes I feel like I'm a character in a novel blending Orwell and Huxley. *Huxwellian.* Perfect adjective. But I understand you leaving. Is Astrid coming with you?"

Tarek nodded.

"Yes, it's easier for her than for Leila. She's a dentist. She can work anywhere. Much tougher for journalists. What's more, the university will help with her work permit."

The Nordic goddess of winter came back with the cognacs. Lee found his tasted strangely bitter. But maybe it was his soul he was tasting instead.

Leila.

Leila was nearly finished revising her questions when her mobile rang. She silently cursed as she was going live in fifteen minutes and had no time to waste. She picked it up anyway and looked at the screen. At first she had thought it was Lee, but she didn't recognize the number. Frowning, she lifted the phone up to her ear.

"Allô?"

"Allô? Miss Leila Bogossian?"

The voice sounded very vaguely familiar, but she couldn't place it. Someone's mother, perhaps?

"Yes?"

"Ingrid Nielsen. I am calling on behalf of miss Kepler, about your book project on her father."

Leila's heart jump-started behind her ribs. That was the old hag at the other end of the line, Marta Kepler's secretary.

"Yes?"

"Miss Kepler would like to meet you. But first you will have to sign some papers I have sent to your email and return them to me, at this address."

She said the address in a robot-like tone, as if she had suddenly morphed into a machine. Which was actually quite plausible. Leila noted it down on a post-it.

"Once this is done, you will receive a formal appointment."

"Oh, thank y . . . "

The hag had hung up. Of course. Power didn't need any politeness.

"Have you looked over the questions?"

Lene's voice gave her a start.

"Yes, of course. I've just finished."

"Good. You're on in five minutes. And remember—this is only because Jakob is sick. Don't get any funny ideas . . . "

Jakob was the "star" anchorman of VCTV 2 Local. Another prick. But with this phone call, she knew she might have her revenge soon. She

would become Shiva the Destroyer. Or Kali, more likely. Whatever. She didn't care for religion. She only cared for herself. Which was sort of a religion, anyway. She stood up to meet her guest and winked at Sheryl Boncoeur's photograph, which she used as her screen background.

Dear Diary.

The trip inside the hollow earth was amazing. April 1937. I will always remember it. That incredible architecture, made of huge arks and colonnades. How I wish Speer could have come with us. I showed him the drawings later and I can see they inspired him. Everything shone blue, crystalline. Pure light from within. We didn't speak. We understood. They told us to try this on the surface, then they would come back. We tried. We failed. The world is not pure enough. Not beautiful enough. Yet.

LEE JR.

Lee had basically the entire idea of the book written down, plus the first two chapters, and had sent the whole thing to his agent. Bill was actually more than his agent—he had become his best friend. For his first novel, Lee had chosen Ed Watkins, the same agent as his father (with his recommendation, which might have helped a lot more than he gave him credit for)—a nice, elderly man who hid his alcoholism behind a fake tan and a tweed jacket—but for Lee, it was too close to home—incestuous, almost. He had met Bill during the launching of his first book (*Dark Constellations,* first bestseller, actually) and they had ended up watching dawn rise on the New Petersburg Long Beach shore, sharing a bottle of Japanese whisky. At first Bill didn't want to take him as a client, because he knew Ed well. But Ed wasokay with it, probably relieved to have only one Lee to deal with again.

The new novel would be more than just a witch hunt during Nazi Germany now. It would a take place today, with a series of flashbacks. The heroine would now be the granddaughter of Sigrid Wulf and her Gypsy lover. She would also have powers and fight against modern-day Nazis regrouped in a secret society hiding behind the legal front of a huge company, known as the Helios Corporation. A cosmetics firm, illegally experimenting on eternal life—trying to patent jellyfish cells, among other things. All that science-fiction stuff.

The last idea actually came from an article he had found online, about Phoebus Industries which had actually funded research on *Turritopsis dohrnii,* the so-called "immortal jellyfish." He had to check with Bill to see if that might cause some legal problems if he kept this in his novel. Given the image he would give of the Helios Corporation, Phoebus Industries could very well sue him and his publisher. Not good.

Lee shut his laptop and walked to the window, looking down at the street. He felt like going to a bar and drinking tonight. His thoughts naturally drifted to Tarek. He would miss him when he'd be gone. He hated to drink alone.

THEORY OF POWER #5

Ideas are like motion picture images. Flat, black and white and shaky. But they provoke feelings which people mistake for reality. They become controlled by them because they believe in them. And they believe in them because they want to be images too. If you tell people they are in your motion picture film, they will do anything for you. Anything.

Leila.

Detective-Inspector Sigrid Wulff was already sitting on the set, looking beautiful. Leila wondered why such a gorgeous woman had chosen to become a cop. Hell, she could have conquered it all, with those looks— Married rich, slept her way to the top, hypnotized the right persons into giving her their fortune and commit suicide afterwards . . . Leila would have given anything to have her looks. In Viborg City, looking like a Nazi Goddess would open all the doors. She knew. Lene looked like one too— albeit a lesser one. A Valkyrie maybe. With small breasts. She smiled to herself and stepped forward to greet her guest.

What Beauty Is.

Good morning, sunny face!

SIGRID.

So the interview had been a catastrophe, of course. Why couldn't she keep her big mouth shut, just once? She had explained that no, there wasn't any indication of Leftist terrorism, as there hadn't been any indication of a Muslim, Gypsy, Black terror action before. That it was all media and political hype and that the police were just trying to do their job, which was made more difficult because of these rumors and the endless number of denunciation phone calls they implied.

The journalist had been nice enough not to insist too much—no "Who do YOU think is behind this?" "What can YOU do to crack this case?" questions—but Sigrid could see she had been somewhat taken aback by her answers. Not used to hearing the truth, apparently. The journalist who had interviewed her, Leila something, had looked familiar and Sigrid had suddenly remembered seeing her on the scene of the crime. Local news, like she was the local cop. Small fry. Not interesting enough for the national channels. But if —*if*—she cracked the case, then Møltke would be all over the screens.

Actually, to her surprise, the man had congratulated her on her performance—behind the closed door of his office. "Good to hear the truth, for once," he had said. Hard to figure out, the boss. Couldn't say she liked him, couldn't say she disliked him. Not like that idiot Jørgensen. The cretin hadn't spoken to her for the rest of the day, like some of her colleagues. Had she hurt a nerve, maybe? Smirking for herself, she pushed through the door of her favorite bar. Henry waved at her from behind the counter, like an old friend. That man was a darling.

Dog Poem #7

We are faithful
To the owners
Who beat us
The most

Leila.

In the subway home, Leila was feeling both tired and excited. She had printed the legal papers, signed them and sent them back to Marta Kepler's robot secretary. She wondered how long she would have to wait. It was true that revenge was a meal best eaten cold, but she felt impatient to see Lene and Jan's faces when they would learn she had actually *met* Marta Kepler.

Ha!

The interview with that cop had gone weird, though. She had expected the standard official bullshit, and she had been met by a political rant against the politicians and the media. She had almost felt like Sheryl Boncoeur for a minute, the queen of the unexpected. Lene had been happy though—unexpected is always good publicity. But Leila hadn't been ready for that, and hadn't hidden her surprise very well. At least, she didn't think so herself. And that was disappointing. She should have been on top, all the time. That cop had revealed her weakness, her *naiveté*. In a way, she felt grateful: she knew now. And she could be thankful for Lene for having given her the test. Lene was satisfied, good for her. But Leila wasn't. Far from it. If she wanted to reach the top, surprise had to be written off her list. Forever.

Sigrid.

"Good job!" Henry said, as he placed her cocktail in front of her

"How do you mean?" she replied, surprised.

"Your interview on TV, this afternoon. I didn't know you were a cop."

For a second, she thought his smile was ironic, but no, his eyes were actually quite warm and friendly.

"We watched it with my friends, completely by chance: Just opened the bar, turned on the TV and there you were."

Sigrid shrugged, not knowing what to answer.

"And if you don't mind me saying so, me and my friends agreed about what you said about the investigation. I think you're barking up the wrong tree. But then again, maybe that was the point all along."

Now Henry had really caught Sigrid's attention. She took a sip of her drink and took a good look at him

"What is it you are suggesting exactly?"

Henry suddenly looked embarrassed.

"I'm not criticizing you, of course. I'm just saying that there are other possibilities. But maybe you've checked them already, what do we know, uh?"

He let out a little nervous laugh.

Sigrid shook her head.

"Henry, I am not angry at all, I'm just not understanding a word you're saying."

"Okay," he said, moving closer as if somebody might be listening to them, although they were the only ones in the bar.

She he had come in early and people would not be coming before an hour or so, after dinner. She had had a fast kebab at the corner Samarqandi, wanting to begin drinking as early as possible. Tomorrow was Saturday; she could sleep late and nurse a hangover.

"What do you know about Niels Kepler?," he asked maliciously.

"That he was a provocative neo-Nazi prick, who could do and say what he pleased because he was filthy rich."

Henry nodded.

"And . . . ?"

"And that he had many enemies."

"And . . . ?"

"And what?"

"That's it? That's all you know?"

Sigrid mentally reviewed all the files and interviews she had gone through and done the past month.

"Yes, I guess so."

Henry moved even closer.

"What about his love life?"

Sigrid's mind rattled like an engine running on empty.

"We checked. Nothing. We did *chercher la femme*, first thing. But zero luck. Seems like Hans was a hardcore bachelor. Or a monk."

"What about *chercher l'homme*?"

Sigrid's mind immediately found some of that missing fuel. *Could it be that simple?*

"You have to tell me more."

"Well, you know my friends, those who come once in a while for a drink a chat. One of them, Ken, used to be a skinhead. A Nazi skinhead, the real deal. And Niels, who used to come to some of their parties, made a pass at him one night. Ken, who didn't know he was gay then, punched him. Apparently, it is a well-known fact that Niels liked young handsome White-Power guys. Like you said on TV, there is no proof that the murder is politically motivated. Disgruntled lovers exist in both sexes . . . That's just my thought, and you can do what you want with it. But I thought you should know."

Sigrid nodded, not knowing what to say. She was saved by two couples walking in. Talking loudly and laughing, they sat at the bar, a few stools away from her. She was planning to get drunk, but she was going to have to go back to her office and check some things out.

6. ELEVEN WAYS TO BURN MORE CALORIES.

Leila was so nervous she felt like throwing up, which would have been tragic, considering the shiny white leather sofa she was sitting in. She could picture herself gagging and spraying some green stuff all over the armrest. Argh. She could vividly imagine Ingrid Nielsen, the Zombie chaperone, picking up the ancient samurai sword displayed on the XVIIIth century commode Leila was facing and beheading her in a swift and elegant gesture. The underpaid personnel would clean up and dispose of her body and her name would be erased from all records. The crazy thoughts made her feel a little better and she tried to relax.

The mansion was huge, sitting in the middle of a park surrounded by a double wall. Leila had no idea such mansions existed in Viborg City, right in the middle of White City. She had seen the walls before, with the CCTV cameras at each corner, but she had assumed it protected some kind of official building, like an embassy or a secret government project. She had never imagined it could have been a private property.

Ingrid had buzzed her in at the gate, and she had walked a long five minutes on a trail through a well-kept park until she had reached the huge blinding-white XVIIIth century mansion. She hadn't seen any bodyguards, but there were video cameras all over the place. They were probably watching her every move, ready to snipe her down anytime.

The mummy had let her in, asked for her mobile phone, and made her sit on that white leather couch. Ingrid had then disappeared through a side-door, leaving her alone and listening to the heavy ticking of an old bronze clock in this incredible rococo antechamber.

The side-door suddenly opened again, startling Leila.

"Miss Kepler will see you now," Ingrid said, in that idiosyncratically monotone voice.

Leila stood up. She hoped the old hag would not notice her trembling hands. She didn't want to appear vulnerable in front of her. Or in front of Marta Kepler, for that matter.

SIGRID.

Chercher l'homme. Easier said than done, apparently. Sigrid had requested all the files on the extreme nationalist movements Niels Kepler had been known to be close to, to no avail. "Classified." She had spent the last three days trying to move forward, explaining the new lead to various higher-ups in different services, but faced a wall. This was very strange. To say the least. But if the official channels didn't want to help her, maybe the unofficial would. She would just have to give them something in exchange.

THEORY OF POWER #6:

Keep them guessing, but make them believe that they know.

LEE JR.

Carlo's coffee was delicious, as usual. The strong smell floated in the small bookstore, fighting with the early afternoon sun to grab attention. They were sitting next to the counter, surrounded by a colorful jungle of books.

"Ever thought of leaving Viborg City?" Lee asked, sipping carefully from his cup to avoid spilling on some second-hand paperback.

Carlo raised his eyebrows in genuine surprise.

"Leave? Why?"

Lee shrugged, thinking about Tarek and wondering what Carlo knew of their friends' plans.

"I don't know. It feels like it's a dead city, sometimes. Culturally, I mean. And politically, well . . . "

"Politically, New Babylon or New Petersburg aren't much better," Carlo said. "And they're actually a model to Viborg City."

Carlo looked around with his melancholic eyes.

"And culturally, well, you might be right. But there is an underground scene that is resisting and doing things. You don't speak Nordic, so you can't know about them."

Lee nodded. It was true that his vision of the city's culture—or lack of—came from a very limited point of view. Couldn't argue with Carlos there. Maybe he only needed to express his own frustration, as he had just done.

"And how are the Nazis treating you, my friend?"

Lee smiled.

"Very well, thank you. I found the plot and began working on the first chapters. Actually, some of it is inspired by one of your famous people. Marta Kepler."

Carlo's eyes shone briefly with a flash of curiosity.

"Oh yes? What about her?"

Lee told his friend what he had discovered in his research and Carlo had a strange smile, caressing his chin as if he wanted to elongate it.

"Very interesting and I am sure your novel will be unofficially banned here. Ignored, like. Or barely mentioned, in some small column of a paper, as the worst bestseller you ever wrote. Dangerous stuff, you're dealing with. You are not going to use her name, right?"

Lee shook his head.

"No, of course. I can't risk legal problems."

"Or your life."

Lee looked for the usual glimmer of irony in Carlo's eyes, but found none.

"How do you mean?"

Carlo stirred his coffee with an old spoon.

"There have been stories. A journalist who became too curious about some of Phoebus Industries' researches and their political implications. Committed suicide. A couple of other things too. Like accidents, organized bad luck and stuff. Nothing ever proven, of course. But you're really dealing with the Evil Empire here. Just so you know."

"I know. That's precisely why I'm using her in my Nazi novel. She's perfect."

"That's the least you can say," Carlo agreed. "And that's not even close."

Leila.

After following Frau Nielsen through what felt like a maze of corridors, they arrived at a nondescript small door.

"Miss Kepler's office," the living dead explained before knocking sharply twice.

She opened the door without waiting for an answer, stepping aside to let Leila in. The room was small too, and bathed in an eerie half-darkness, as a heavy curtain were drawn over a narrow window. An old fashioned desk stood on the opposite side, looking huge because of the narrowness of the walls. A figure sat behind it, its face barely lit by a laptop's screen. There was also a chair and a large bookshelf that covered the wall behind the desk. The door behind her slammed shut, and Leila felt her heart jump behind her rib-cage.

"Sit down, please."

The voice was nice and melodious, strangely youthful. Quite a change from Frau Nielsen's. Leila wondered if that was part of a constructed act, like "god cop, bad cop", with Frau Nielsen and Marta Kepler as a complementary couple.

Leila obeyed and sat down on the chair. She felt like a schoolgirl who had been summoned by the principal.

"So, Miss Bogossian, I understand you would like to write a biography about my father . . . May I ask you why?"

Leila had expected that question and had rehearsed her answer in her head over and over.

"I think your father was an incredible personality, and that people need to know about him. After all, he is the epitome of a self-made man, and should be regarded as a role-model to all."

Leila heard the tapping of fingertips.

"You know how about his past, don't you? I mean . . . before he arrived in Viborg City?"

Leila nodded.

"Yes, and that's why I would like to write his biography. From being

Hitler's perfumer to the founder of one of the world's largest cosmetics corporation—what a dedication to beauty . . . "

Leila felt, more than saw, Marta smile.

"Dedication to beauty. I like that. That's exactly what it was about. And still is."

There was a pause, which seemed a century long for Leila.

"Okay, I will let you write it. But this project must remain secret until it is finished. You will have more papers to sign. And you will have to show me everything you write. Everything, is that clear?"

"Of course. I understand perfectly well."

"Frau Nielsen will give you access to the family archives, at least to my father's. Do you speak or read German?"

Leila shook her head.

"Okay, I will commission someone who can translate what you need to read—but it cannot be any personal correspondence. Only the official stuff."

"I understand."

"Very well, then. It's a deal. You will receive the contract and legal papers next week."

The door opened as if by magic, and Frau Nielsen stepped in, like an automaton. Leila stood up and followed the old secretary one more time through the maze, until they reached the main door.

It was only when she was back in the street that Leila began to shake uncontrollably. But it was because she was laughing with relief.

SIGRID.

It wasn't very long since she had seen Carlo, and she wondered what his reaction would be. Their paths had crossed a couple of times during the years, each time there was a case linked with some underground leftist group. Carlo was a well-known radical figure, who discreetly supported leftist youth organizations by selling their home-printed manifestos in his second-hand bookstore. The government suspected him of being involved in more illegal actions, but this had never been proven. Every time Sigrid had met him, he had been courteous and helpful, if there was some degree of unacceptable violence involved— she knew, from other sources, that Carlo was a hardcore pacifist, who never condoned any terror action. He had even pointed her in the direction of a small but ultra-violent group who was planning a few bombings in Viborg City. Although she had never mentioned Carlo's part in the arrests, she knew the city owed him a big one. The same was true with Kepler's murder—he had told her that he didn't think any Samarqandi or leftist organization had anything to do with it. And he had been right.

Now she was going to ask him about connecting him to hackers, which could be a completely different story. Those networks were even more secretive than terror organizations. She would have to prove convincing.

She pushed the door of the bookstore and was welcomed by the smell of freshly brewed coffee and the sound of a quiet conversation. Shit. He wasn't alone. She moved forward between the book shelves. Carlo sat with a handsome young man with short dark hair and glasses, discussing in English. The bookseller noticed her and stood up to politely greet her.

"Detective-inspector Wulff, Lee Jones Jr. He's a writer. And she's, well . . . a cop."

The young man smiled and extended a hand. She took it and found it surprisingly firm.

"I have to admit it's quite incredible meeting you," the writer said in

New Babylonian English. "You have inspired the main character of my new novel!"

Sigrid raised a surprised elbow, not knowing how to take this.

"I hope you don't mind," Jones Jr. resumed." I saw you on TV because of that Kepler murder thing and I thought you looked just like the heroine of my story. A young woman fighting Nazis."

The detective-inspector smiled in spite of herself.

"That sounds *quite à propos*," she said. "I would love to read it sometime."

"I'll send you a signed copy."

Carlo looked at her with serious eyes.

"You wanted to see me?" he said, in Nordic.

Sigrid nodded, professional again.

"Yes. It won't take long."

The writer stood up, as if he had understood their conversation.

"I'll leave you guys to your conspiracy. Thanks for the coffee, Carlo."

Carlo nodded.

"My pleasure. Always good talking to you."

"And very nice to meet you, Mrs. Wulff. Do you have a card, by chance?"

Slightly taken aback, she looked at him defensively.

"My card? Why?"

"So I can send you a signed copy."

"He is quite a famous writer, outside of our city," Carlo explained. "Writes bestsellers actually."

"Oh," Sigrid said, feeling a little stupid. "I don't read much."

"And you have a good excuse," Carlo said. "He's never been translated into Nordic—which is a shame. Probably too political . . . Or cultured . . . We were actually talking about that . . . "

"I see," Sigrid said. "Then I would probably like your books, Mister Jones. Here's my card. And its Miss, not Mrs."

The young writer took and card with a mock bow and left the shop, zigzagging between the shelves. She was surprised to have found him handsome. For a writer.

Dear Diary.

To live in secrets, to hide within one self—that is the fate of the greatest. If you can survive wearing a mask forever, then you are truly one of the chosen. Beauty reaches both ways—inside and outside. And beauty is strength. Absolute strength. Nothing can resist beauty. Not even strength.

7. THE LONGEST LASTING NAIL POLISH YOU CAN BUY IS ALSO THE CHEAPEST

Leila looked at the files piling up on her table in the middle of the living room. Soon their two-room apartment would be too small. *Maybe Lee should find himself another place*, she joked to herself. But it was not so funny. The last three weeks had been difficult, to say the least. She felt she had been engulfed in a gigantic quicksand of work, both at the TV station and at home. She would work her normal shift, then come back to the apartment and read through pages and pages of documentation about Marta Kepler's father. Most of it were official files, translated by the OSS in 1945, but some of them were also letters and notebooks—with a translated transcript she had been given.

Leila had been surprised at first, as Marta had told her that she would not see personal papers. She had thought she might have been given the papers by mistake, but an email exchange with Marta had reassured her: Marta had trusted her and had given her a "little more" than had been agreed. Leila had felt touched by the attention. It was a sign of trust, something Lene would never give her at work.

She was working on a rough draft, in three sections—before the war, during the war, after the war. If this was going to be a bestseller, it had to remain simple. What had emerged through the hundreds of pages she had read was that Kepler Senior had been an idealistic young man, fascinated by beauty and death. His own mother—who had been very beautiful, Leila had seen the copy of a photograph—had died young, and he had apparently missed her very much. Her name had been Maria, and that was also the name of the first cologne he had created, and which was to become one of Eva Braun's favorite. He had dabbled in the occult in the 20s and the 30s, joining the infamous Black Sun Society in 1929, to which Himmler himself had belonged. Lee had been right on that point, she had to admit. It was actually through him that Kepler Senior had been introduced to the Führer, although he had never formally

joined the Nazi party, as his 1945 OSS discharge proved. And that was also where he had met his wife, Maria, in 1933—who incidentally had the same name as his mother—and his perfume. The only picture of her that Leila had got was the same that could be found on the net—she wondered if others existed. And the resemblance to Marta was uncanny. They really looked like the same person.

What made this all the more eerie was that there no birth attests of Marta and her brother. Marta said she was born in 1939 and her brother in 1944 but that all the papers burned in the bombing of their house in Berlin, which was also where her mother died. Not a trace of their childhood either, nothing before the first few and only pictures in the 1980s, when she was in her early 40s. She should have been in her 70s now, and her brother in his 60s. He appeared to be in his early 40s. And her? Leila had never seen her face, but her voice definitely wasn't old. Yet another mystery.

Maybe the Phoebus rejuvenation product line did work miracles after all . . . She sighed and opened another file.

SIGRID.

Sigrid lifted her eyes from the listings of the extreme right group members she had finally obtained through Carlo's contact. She blinked a couple times, to make them water. She now understood why the Secret Police didn't want her to have access. Some of her colleagues were on those lists. Jørgensen himself was in one of those associations—not the most radical, but a nationalist group nonetheless. He had been a member a good decade. No wonder he had been so hostile. Her union representative was in the same group. He might have tipped Jørgensen on her. Wonderful.

The three weeks of negotiations had been worth it after all. What she had to give them in exchange was small, but extremely dangerous: her address and her Persocard number. They could track her anytime and anywhere. She was completely transparent for them, and should they be displeased with her, they could destroy her completely overnight—by emptying her bank account, making her personal files public, sending insulting emails in her name to various people, etc.

Sigrid had not met any of the people hiding behind the Potemkin Crew Redux, as they called themselves in reference to the mythical original Potemkin Crew, that had managed to hack into a New Babylonian military coalition satellite during the South-East Chinese War. Even Carlo didn't know who they were, or so he said—she wouldn't check anyway. She liked the guy, and he had done her a huge favor by putting her in contact and vouching for her. It was fortunate they were on the same side. Sigrid actually wondered if she should ask to join them. After all, they were the only ones fighting for justice, in a strange illegal way.

They had also sent her a compressed file full of photographs, both private and public, with name tags. Some of them obviously came from police surveillance and she wondered if they had been stolen, or if some cop had sent them. She liked the second possibility better, because it made her feel less alone.

Sigrid stood up and stretched in her tiny sitting-room. She suddenly realized that she had never written an e-mail to Marta Kepler, asking to meet her. Maybe her brain had subconsciously decided that it was a dead end anyway. Which it probably was. But still, she would confront the rich bitch. Just for her own honor's sake.

She rubbed her eyes, which hurt from staring too long at her laptop's screen in the half-darkness of her apartment. She had pulled the curtains to avoid the neighbors' curiosity. Viborg City had the highest rate in the world of anonymous tips to the police and the tax department. One was never too careful.

She sighed over the sorry state of her own city and stretched. She needed a drink now—and a stiff one.

What Beauty Is.

Light up your smile
With sparkle and style!

LEE JR.

Although it was a warm Nordic spring evening, with small yellow clouds drifting slowly across a hard blue sky, Lee was feeling very depressed. The good weather actually made things worse. The Sorgbjerg façades looked like a film décor, a Potemkin city built to make one forget the social misery and oppression it actually contained. Lee just had had a drink with a young student from the School of Journalism who had bought one of his novels in the airport coming home from some vacation in some warm country. The kid had read it in one long sitting in the overcrowded plane and had been struck by literary lightning. He had found Lee's contact on the net and had asked to meet him for an interview. During the hour and half they had spent together drinking beer in that café, his recurring question had been, "But why aren't you more known here?" It was more of an accusation, actually, than a question, as if Lee had failed somehow.

Bill had tried several times to sell the books to various Viborg City publishers, to no avail. "It wouldn't interest the audience here" was the usual reply. Now, he actually knew why—nothing interested Viborg City outside of Viborg City. Every time a celebrity from Babylon or Petersburg was interviewed here, they were asked what they thought of Viborg City. As if it mattered.

The kid had depressed him, but he was just a symptom. This whole city was depressing him, and worse than that, it was killing his relationship. The happy, easy-going, open-minded Leila he had met in Babylon was becoming a stressed-out, ambitious bitch. He immediately regretted the word, but it had blown up in his mind like a flash-bang grenade.

The fact was that they were not communicating anymore, and that Lee felt he was dangerously following his father's drunken steps— nothing a couple pints couldn't cure, until the next day. The hangovers blended with Leila's physical absence during the day, and her mental absence in the evenings. "Listen, this book is really important to me,"

she would tell him, as if *his* books were less important—and he was the writer in the couple! What was more, she seemed to find excuses to talk about that Nazi bastard she was writing about. "There were very complicated times, we can't understand, we can't really judge . . . " It was as if that woman, Marta Kepler, had poisoned her mind somehow, killing all her critical sense. He accepted Leila's focus on her revenge upon her boss and work, but why did she have to accept all those pathetic "explanations" she was being fed with a golden spoon?

During their last fight, as recent as this morning, he had told her that with her skin color, she would have been one of the first in Viborg City to be sent to a concentration camp. She had glared at him and replied: "Things were different then." Yes, precisely. And not better now, it seemed. A bar window caught his eye. He noticed a beautiful blonde sitting alone on a bar-stool, chatting with the bartender. She looked vaguely familiar. He felt like drinking and talking to someone. The image of his father crossed his mind as he pulled the door open.

THEORY OF POWER #6

The harmony of colors is essential and white has to be in the center, always in the center. White is the mother of all colors and the great eraser. It is the supreme harmony, the lost paradise and the future garden of Eden. The harmony must be preserved, even if it means destroying all other colors. And I mean ALL other colors.

SIGRID.

It had taken her a while to recognize him. The writer. He had sat next to her and had ordered a drink. He had told her who he was, that they had briefly met at Carlo's and that's when she remembered him. The handsome writer. They had chatted and shared drinks and stories. Some stories. She realized she liked him. There was something vulnerable about him, something dark and secret. The mysterious stranger from Babylon. She told him about the political situation in Viborg City—he seemed interested. That was nice, for a change. They drank some more and she felt very much like kissing him when they parted, around two in the morning. Now that she was home, in her empty bed, she was wondering if he had felt the same way.

Dear Diary.

Little by little, we are progressing. And we don't have to do anything. No one can resist the truth offered by beauty. No one. Not even our worst enemies. And they are helping us now spread the word. Converted without even realizing it. A master plan. Beauty is a deadly virus. Maybe the deadliest of all.

8. STRENGTH THROUGH JOY.

Leila walked into the dimly lit office, her heart beating against her throat. She had sent the first draft of Hans Kepler's biography to Marta about three weeks ago, but hadn't heard anything until Frau Nielsen's phone call last night, telling her to come at eight in the evening today. Distinguishing the frail silhouette behind the desk, Leila felt that all of her future lay in the next seconds to come.

"Ah. Leila, you're here! I can call you Leila, yes?"

The familiarity and joyfulness of the voice lifted an enormous weight off Leila's shoulders. If she had been Sheryl Boncoeur, she would have asked for an interview, right here, right now, with her cell phone camera. But the image of Sheryl was fading now, replaced by a stranger one: her own face, smiling nervously.

"Yes, yes, of course, Miss Kepler."

"Call me Marta. And sit down, please."

Leila felt her knees grow weak and was happy to find the firmness of the seat.

"That book . . . "

Leila saw the two hands tap on the pile of white pages. They looked incredibly young.

"That book, Leila, is the most wonderful book I have read in a long, long time."

The hands stroked the cover as if it were made of precious metal.

"You have understood everything about Hans. I felt he was near me again, talking to me, telling me about his dreams. You don't know how much that means to me . . . "

Leila felt a warm sun rise inside her chest.

"I tried to do your father justice. He was a man who loved beauty and wanted the world to share it. Hitler was only an accident, in a way."

"Yes, exactly!" the silhouette exclaimed, suddenly excited. "I couldn't have said it better myself!"

There was a longue pause, during which Leila could hear her own heartbeat. It was then she noticed the faint, but wonderful smell surrounding her. She wondered what perfume Marta was wearing. It was as if she was standing under a summer shower during a really hot day.

"I want to know," the voice continued, "if you can keep a secret. On your life."

Leila nodded without thinking. Lene and Jan would sell their souls for a moment like this.

"Of course. You've read my book: I've done everything as you asked me to."

"When I say 'on your life,' I mean it, Leila."

The voice was still playful, but Leila understood the real threat behind it.

"Of course," she repeated.

She had to ask Marta the name of that perfume, although she knew she could never afford it.

"Only my governess knows it too. And my brother. But he is dead now."

No sadness in her voice. Just a statement.

"You don't have to It's that simple. But I trust you and feel that you might be the friend I have been looking for all those years. Finally."

Leila didn't know if she was dreaming or if this was for real. She buried a nail into her palm. No, it was real.

She saw the silhouette reach for the desk lamp and turn it toward herself. Leila gasped. It was the exact same woman from the picture taken in the 70s, and the one from the 1930s.

"There is no Marta, Leila. I am Maria Sizic. I am immortal. Hans wasn't my father. He was my husband."

THEORY OF POWER #7

Absolute power is absolute beauty.

Absolute beauty is absolute power.

They are both merciless, and nothing else is worth living for.

Absolutely nothing.

SIGRID.

Møltke looked again at the pile of printed pages Sigrid had dropped on his desk.

"I don't know," he said. "These are very grave accusations. Are you 100% sure?"

Sigrid nodded, trying to find his eyes, which seemed to look for cracks on the walls and ceiling of his office.

"We can send for him and ask him for a DNA sample. I have at least three witnesses who can put him on the motorbike that day, I know who sold him the gun and we have the motive—which is passion, as crazy as it may seem. Niels had dumped him for another boyfriend—he will testify too, he told me."

Møltke scratched its bald head.

"But Niels Kepler was always surrounded by beautiful women. Models, most of them."

"Probably to put up a front. We can ask them too."

Møltke sighed.

"This is very thin evidence. I am not sure that . . . "

Sigrid crossed her arms across her chest.

"Of course, I can always go to the press. They would love that."

Møltke shook his head, forcing a thin smile.

"No, no, no, no need for that. But you understand the implications of your accusation. And you know who Marta Kepler is, what she represents. Phoebus Industries is . . . "

"The beating heart of this this city, a friend of the royal family and a basket-case who never shows herself in public. Yes, I know perfectly well who she is. As well as we all know that Niels Kepler was supporting extreme-right movements, which is a nice word to say Neo-Nazis."

"Niels Kepler was not a Nazi," Møltke protested. "You can't call him that."

There was an awkward silence. During which Sigrid wondered if she shouldn't have gone to the media directly.

"Ok, we'll call him in and take a DNA sample. That's all I can do right now."

"And what about the list?"

Møltke seemed to wake up from a trance.

"Ah yes. Where did you get it?"

"It doesn't matter where I got it. I think you should forward it to Internal Affairs. There are many colleagues on this list. Something should be done. Jørgensen himself is on it. It concerns you directly then."

"I will contact Internal Affairs. And thank you for the good work, Detective-Inspector Wulff. We need more like you in our ranks."

He smiled a strange, anguished smile, and Sigrid noticed his collar was wet with sweat. Truth always made people hot and uneasy. And she would go to the media anyway. You could never trust the police, as she knew so well.

LEE JR.

Tarek was very drunk and very happy. It was actually the first time that Lee had seen anybody really happy in this city, and that was because he was leaving.

"We've got our tickets and we are leaving in three weeks. You should do the same, my friend. This city is poison. Really, really bad poison."

Lee nodded vaguely, thinking about Leila. They were in the bar where he had met Sigrid Wulff. He had told Tarek they should meet here. "Great cocktails," he said, which was only half of the story. Of course, he still loved Leila. Things had been better since she had finished her book. Made love in the morning even, which was always a good sign. And then again—Sigrid had moved something in his heart, which was more than desire. Maybe it had been her melancholy, or her cynicism. Or both. She had felt . . . real. That was the word. Real.

Everything in this city felt artificial, as if it didn't exist. The king, the rich, the poor, the immigrants, morals, work, passion, everything was thin air. And he choked on it. Sigrid had been an evening of pure oxygen, and he couldn't forget her because of that. That's how she would shine in his novel.

"Cheers, my friend," Tarek said, lifting his glass. "You were right about this place: fantastic cocktails. Fantastic!"

Dog Poem #8

We piss everywhere
Because *we* can

SIGRID.

Sigrid heard her doorbell ring first in her dream, then for real when she finally awoke. She glanced at her alarm clock and wondered who wanted to see her at three thirty in the morning. She stood up, took her service gun resting on the chair, and quickly tiptoed to the door of her apartment. Looking through the peeping hole, she recognized Jørgensen, but his face was covered with a self-tanning cream and he wore a black wig. What was going on? Was she still dreaming? She half-opened the door and saw a black thing hovering over her eyes. It took her a fraction of a second too long to identify the silencer.

Dear Diary.

We are moving forward again. I can feel it. More will follow and beauty will rise They will come back, and the world will again be made of steel and sunshine. A different world, this time, because everybody will want to be part of it. Everybody will want to be beautiful.

Leila.

Leila was floating on a pink cloud. She had officially resigned from her position, explaining to Lene that she was now going to be Marta Kepler's personal assistant. She had been waiting for this moment for so long that she almost didn't register her ex-boss's gaping mouth. And she hadn't even told her about the book, coming out next fall. *Double-whammy*, she smiled to herself, as she walked toward her car. She had left Lene's office without looking back once, like in a Clint Eastwood film. Goodbye Sheryl Boncoeur, goodbye media dreams. There was another yellow brick road ahead, and it was her own to make.

As she sat behind the wheel, she remembered all the crazy stuff Marta had told her the last time they had met—about the Nazi black magic séances, her visit to Aryan aliens who were living in the center of the earth, the immortality they had granted her and the mission that came with it . . . Marta had even showed her Himmler's secret diary, in which he wrote weird poems about magic and power . . . She didn't know if she should believe all of this or dismiss it as the ranting of a lunatic. Maybe Marta was just Maria's secret granddaughter, or a sly impostor, or really Maria Sizic, an immortal Nazi goddess—who knew? And who cared, right?

Shrugging, she started the car. There was a new anti-aging product from Phoebus Industries to be presented tonight to the media. Her first job for Marta. And this was what counted now. This, and nothing else.

LEE JR.

If he hadn't been eating in front of the TV, he would have missed the info. A one minute flash, just before the sports news. Sigrid Wulff's face appeared in the background, in a police uniform. His bad Nordic was good enough to understand that she had been murdered, and that a Gypsy was the prime suspect. Arrests were being made. Border controls were tightened. "Terror" was mentioned several times. New restrictive laws were on the way. This obviously had happened while he had been out with Tarek: she had become a ghost while he was getting drunk. His thoughts drifted to his novel. There would be a story behind the story. The readers would love that. He could hear his father: "Fiction has no more soul than reality." And once again, unfortunately, he would be right. He would be right.

What Beauty Is.

Throw out
Your makeup
Now

ABOUT THE AUTHOR

Sébastien Doubinsky is a bilingual French writer and academic, born in Paris in 1963. An established writer in France, Sébastien Doubinsky has published a series of novels, covering different genres, from classical literature to crime fiction, as well as a few poetry collections. His novels, *The Babylonian Trilogy* (*Goodbye Babylon* in the US), *The Song of Synth* and *Absinth* have been published in the UK and the US. Three of his poetry collections, *Mothballs, Spontaneous Combustions*, and *Zen and the Art of Poetry Maintenance* have been published in the UK. He currently lives in Denmark, where he teaches French literature, culture and history at the French department of the university of Aarhus.

All Art is Junk by R. A. Harris

Lana Rivers, a girl with paintbrush hair, is missing and it's up to Lancelot, her cyborg knight, and his bionic conjoined twin, Cilia, to find her before her evil father, a disrespected artist turned mad-scientist, performs a terrible experiment on her.

Cherub by David C. Hayes

Cherub wasn't like the other boys—too slow, too rough—but he didn't deserve what that hospital did to him, and now he will make them pay.

Skinners by Adam Millard

Los Angeles, the City of Angels. At least, that's what the brochure says. What it fails to mention is the earthquakes. Oh, and the flesh-eating creatures lying dormant beneath the concrete, waiting for the chance to surface once again. Their wait is over . . .

The After-Life Story of Pork Knuckles Malone by MP Johnson

What's a farm boy to do when his pet pig becomes an evil, decaying hunk of ham with slime-spewing psychic powers?

A Lightbulb's Lament by Grant Wamack

A gentleman with a lightbulb for head wakes up in a world full of darkness, hooks up with a beautiful ex-prostitute, and an old man who can heal people; he travels down south to find the mysterious Creator.

The Horror Show by Vincenzo Bilof

A poetry novel—a narcoleptic, amnesiac Nobel Prize-winning poet becomes the subject of an experiment to cure madness.

Beyond by Jordan Krall

From Jerusalem to Mars, psychiatry and the unraveling of the universe

Gravity Comics Massacre
by Vincenzo Bilof

An absolutely shitty novella involving comic books, aliens, a serial killer, teenagers in an abandoned town, horror-trope dream sequences, and an ending you're going to hate.

Glue by Scott Lange

Sticky bowels and sticky situations.

Ascent by Matthew Bialer

Is the 8 foot tall creature haunting a small town in Iowa in the fall of the year 1903 the product of a hoax and collective imagination or was it one of the first documented paranormal event in America? This epic poem grapples with these questions.

Fecal Terror by David Bernstein

A killer turd is on the loose!

The Fairy Princess of Trains
by Christopher Boyle

Danny's mediocre life turns upside-down when his couch starts whispering to him. Then he's charged with a supernatural mission: Rescue the Fairy Princess of Trains.

Terence, Mephisto & Viscera Eyes
by Chris Kelso

9 new science fiction stories from Chris Kelso

How to Succesfully Kidnap Strangers by Max Booth III

Do not respond to bad reviews. If you must respond to bad reviews, please do not kidnap the reviewer.

Bizarro Bizarro: An Anthology

The finest bizarro short stories from 2013.

Necrosaurus Rex by Nicolas Day

Necrosaurus Rex tells the tale of Martin, a simple janitor, who takes an unfortunate trip through time, becomes a violent mutant, and the father of us all. There's 14 billion years crushed inside these pages, and most of them are pretty nasty.

Day of the Milkman by S. T. Cartledge

In a world dominated by the milk industry, only one milkman survives after a terrible storm sinks all the ships and throws the Great White Sea out of balance.

Moosejaw Frontier by Chris Kelso

An unapologetic disaster of metafiction

Notes from the Guts of a Hippo by Grant Wamack

A rugged journalist travels to Brazil in search of a missing hippo researcher and the notes left behind lead to something earth shatteringly revelatory.

Industrial Carpet Drag by Bruce Taylor

Chemicals make you do great things!

ADHD Vampire by Matthew Vaughn

He came, he conquered, he was distracted a lot

www.ingramcontent.com/pod-product-compliance
Lightning Source LLC
Chambersburg PA
CBHW050820180626
46814CB00004B/1384